Millie,

Enjoy .... and become a Doughty Warrior too!

Brenda Brott

This book will be popular with both children and adults. Set in a fictitious country in South East Asia, it is full of danger and adventure. It is multi-cultural (involving children from different ethnicities), indigenous people and creatures of the forest.

Six young friends tackle the evil palm oil baron who is burning down the forest to plant palm oil. With help from their parents, villagers, indigenous people and the creatures of the forest, they save the precious forest, and the Prime Minister places a preservation order on it.

A first class story, it has all the elements children love: adventure, slapstick humour, camaraderie and, finally, sweet victory. A David and Goliath theme, it has a strong ecological message, encouraging children to save and preserve the rainforests. "A book to curl up with."

THE
DOUGHTY
WARRIORS

"It's Our Forest Too!"

3.

BRENDA BROSTER

For Oliver, Georgette, & Humphrey.
For your future, and that of your children.

◇◇◇

Printed on FSC (Forest Stewardship Council)
Prima Smooth Cream 80gsm
Not derived from virgin forest

B B Books (Pte.) Ltd

Published in Singapore
By B B Books (Pte.) Ltd

Registered with IP Rights Office
Copyright Registration Service Ref. 1570098550

The moral right of the author has been asserted.

The ISBN for this book has been registered in Singapore and lodged with Nielsen's in the U.K.

Hardback ISBN 978-981-08-3149-3
Paperback ISBN 978-981-08-3342-8

Printed and bound in Singapore by
Ngai Heng Book Binder Pte Ltd.

Papers used by B B Books (Pte.) Ltd. are natural, renewable, and recyclable products sourced from well-managed forests and certified in accordance with the rules of the Forest Stewardship Council.

B B Books (Pte.) Ltd
1 Kaki Bukit Road 1
#02-44 Enterprise One
Singapore 415934

www.Doughtywarriors.com

PREFACE

Brenda has had such fun writing this book! It is full of adventure, struggles of good and evil, wild animals, indigenous people, and, above all, children from different ethnic origins, of different race, colour and religion who are, nonetheless, the best of friends.

Watch children playing together – they never notice skin colour, religious inclinations, or any other difference. It is all taken in their stride in a practical manner. They are simply 'friends'. It is adults who impose restrictions.

It is a fact that the rainforests of the world are, in a sense, the guardians of the world. They absorb carbon dioxide, and produce oxygen for us to breathe. They provide us with shelter, food, and medicines, yet we are destroying them at the rate of fifty football pitches a minute - for every minute of every hour of every day of every week of every month of every year.

When all the rainforests with their rich diversity of life have gone, what then? What will become of our planet? What will become of us? Just as we relentlessly burned the creatures and the precious plants of the forest to death, will we in turn be burned to death by a relentless sun?

If this book encourages future generations to preserve and appreciate the forests, Brenda will have achieved her aim.

She would like to take this opportunity of thanking her darling Martin without whose encouragement she would never have embarked on this book, Dan Poynter, who gave her the courage to publish, Patrick Ang who instigated the marketing of the book with such enthusiasm, Kana Gopal who edited and proof read it, and Shafique Bhaktiar for his delightful illustrations.

This is a work of fiction. Any similarity or resemblance to actual persons, living or dead, is coincidental.

The characters within this book are the creations of the author's imagination.

"The forest is a peculiar organism of unlimited kindness and benevolence, that makes no demands for sustenance, and extends generously the products of its activity; it affords protection to all beings, offering shade even to the axeman who destroys it."

Lord Buddha
500 B.C.

CHAPTER 1

The first day of the summer holidays, it was hot and languid as usual. Joseph, Vinod, and Xin Hui were lying in the sun drying off after their swim when Ibrahim came running up. He was panting, breathless, which was unusual for Ibrahim. He never felt the heat.

"You must come" he shouted, "Come! Come quickly! They're burning the forest".

Joseph, Vinod and Xin Hui threw on their tee-shirts and shorts, slipped into their flip-flops, and jogged at a lope behind Ibrahim. When they got to the edge of the forest, Faradilla, Ibrahim's little sister, was there, waiting for them. She pointed down into the valley. They saw men like ants below, firing the underbrush. They were working along the edge of a wide dirt road cut around the forest boundary. The forest was dry, the tinder sparked, and, in no time at all, the forest was a raging furnace. A heavy smoke pall quickly appeared. There was no wind to blow it away, so it hung over them, making Faradilla cough and choke. The men below drew back, kerchiefs tied over their mouths and noses. They climbed onto their lorry and drove away.

Xin Hui started crying. "What are they doing? Why are they doing this? They're killing everything" she cried.

"We must get down there" Joseph said. "The animals. We must help the animals." They stumbled down the escarpment to the valley below. "Get to the road" he shouted. The fire was crackling, flames roaring, the trees snapping. The noise and the heat were terrible. The smoke was suffocating.

They reached the road where, already, small things were trying desperately to get away from the fire: beetles, ants, moths, butterflies, centipedes and millipedes. Birds were wheeling overhead, screaming. There were lizards trying to escape, but they were slow. Snakes, rats and mice. So many creatures! Then the flying squirrels and flying foxes came hurtling through the trees, along with the shrieking macaques and the gibbons. The children could see a family of orang-utans desperately trying to reach the safety of the road.

"What shall we do?" shouted Vinod.

"Help them" shouted Joseph. He always seemed to take charge. He started scooping up as many insects as he could. He tossed them onto the grassland on the other side of the road, away from the fire. Following his example, all the children swooped down on the animals. Vinod, hiding his fear, picked up a couple of snakes, and dropped them quickly into the grass. Xin Hui and Faradilla concentrated on the lizards and skinks, and Ibrahim ran up and down the road rescuing anything he could, tossing it unceremoniously into the grass on the far side of the road. The macaques and gibbons were quick. They managed to cross on their own, but the orang-utan family was in trouble. One of the babies had fallen into the fire. The rest of the family did not want to leave it, and the fire was raging all around them. They were getting burned. The baby, on the ground, shrieking in distress, was paralysed with fear. Ibrahim saw it.

"Oh no! It's Tunku and his family. Give me your tee-shirt,

Vinod." he shouted. Vinod took off his tee-shirt, threw it at Ibrahim. Ibrahim grabbed it and ran in to the burning forest. He scooped up the baby orang-utan, draped it in the tee-shirt, and ran back to the road. The orang-utan family followed. The baby's little hands and feet were burned, its hair was singed. It was whimpering. Ibrahim carried on running, closely followed by the orang-utans. The terrified animals were screaming, roaring, hooting, gibbering, in fear and in pain.

When he felt safe, Ibrahim turned and sat down, cradling the baby gently in his arms. He examined it carefully, watched closely by the orang-utans. They were concerned, but they made no move to interfere with Ibrahim. If inclined, they could easily have killed him.

"We need help" he said. "It's hands and feet are badly burned, and its body's scalded. It might die of shock, anyway." He handed the tee-shirt back to Vinod. "Thanks." he said.

Ibrahim handed the baby orang-utan to Joseph who, with the girls, was still scooping up the slower creatures and tossing them onto the grassland. Vinod spotted a monitor lizard thrashing about. He seized it with both hands, helping it out. But the lizard was not grateful. Angrily it writhed in his hands. He was struggling to hold it. "Help me" he shouted. Ibrahim ran up, stroked the lizard and, within seconds, it was quiet and malleable. "It's badly burned too" said Ibrahim. "Look at its back and its tail".

Joseph, still cradling the baby orang-utan, called to Ibrahim. "You'll have to tell them, Ibrahim. If it doesn't get help, it'll die. Your father will have to help."

Ibrahim had lived in or close to the forest all his life. He knew it well. He knew all the creatures which dwelled there, and had learned to communicate with them. He spent hours wandering, alone, through the forest, or flying through the trees with Tunku and his family. Sometimes, he would hitch a ride with one of the elephants. He was happier in there than in the rest of the world. The children knew that. He had already told them they should never be frightened in the forest, that the animals understood them and were, frequently, far more frightened, themselves, than the children. He told them they would never be hurt by any of the creatures of the forest. He, Ibrahim, had made them a solemn promise, and it would be kept. They had no cause to doubt him.

Ibrahim went up to the orang-utans. The male was particularly big. His red hair was long, and thickest on his shoulders. His great cheek flaps and throat pouch made his head look enormous. His arms were twice as long as his legs, and when he walked, he used the knuckles of his long arms to propel himself forward. Xin Hui thought he looked quite scary.

"Tunku, if we don't help him" he said "your baby will die from the shock. He's in a lot of pain. I want to take him to my father, who will help him. As soon as he is well, I shall bring him back to you." The flames were still raging, the roar of the fire intense, the smell of burning was terrible. And, even here, some distance away from the flames, the smoke was suffocating.

The orang-utans were silent, as were the other children, all watching, waiting. Eventually the big male smacked his lips, and nodded his great head slowly. Ibrahim breathed a sigh of relief. "It's OK. We can take him to my father" he said. "We'll have to take the monitor too, and some of those others over there". He pointed to an assortment of small, partially burned, sorry little creatures.

In between rescuing animals, the children beat at the flames with all their strength. They used fallen branches, anything they could lift, to beat the flames. But they were weak against the might of the fire.

The fire had been raging for two hours, and the children had done all they could. They were exhausted, dishevelled, smoke-blackened, and coughing up blackened spume. They needed water, a shower, clean clothes, something to eat. They set off, Joseph cradling the baby orang-utan, Vinod cradling the monitor lizard. Xin Hui had gathered up a slow loris and a civet cat, both of which were burned. Ibrahim and Faradilla rounded up as many other hurt creatures as they could which were still able to walk, hop or slither, and carried several which could not move. Faradilla perched a baby gibbon on her shoulder, and carried a civet cat with burned paws in her arms.

They headed for Ibrahim's father's house on the edge of the nearby kampong. He had a large house, and a lot of land. Aishah, his wife, was in charge of the garden. She grew maize, potatoes, pak choi, spinach, onions, tomatoes, leeks, kailan, and cucumbers. She had fruit trees: mango, banana, guava, papaya, durian, mangosteen, rambutan and jack fruit, and a tamarind tree as well. She grew pineapples and strawberries, and collected wild mushrooms from the forest. She had a little paddy field, which grew enough rice to sustain the family, and she had chickens and ducks. There were baby chickens and ducks everywhere, as well as a buffalo, a couple of goats, cats, and a dog called Katak (which means 'frog').

"Why's the dog called Katak?" Xin Hui had asked.

"Because it had legs like a frog's when it was a puppy" said Faradilla.

Ibrahim's father, Yusof, was a man of the forest. He looked after the plants there, the herbs, the animals. A leading pharmacognosist, he knew which herbs and plants to use, to heal, to sooth. He spent most of his time researching the medicinal properties of forest plants. Locally, he was known as a great healer. He would help.

The orang-utans followed the children at a safe distance. They would not let the little baby out of their sight.

At the edge of the kampong, they were met by Ibrahim's father. He, too, was black with soot and grime. He looked grim. "There you are" he said. "I should have known".

"Ayah" Ibrahim said. "You've got to help us. I promised the creatures. They're in such pain." Yusof was gentle. "Leave the animals here" he said. Immediately, he gave them water. Speaking quietly, he told the animals that he would help them as best he could. He, with the help of the children, would attend to their burns, and then water, food, and bedding would be arranged.

Quickly, Yusof organised the children: Ibrahim, who knew the plants of the forest, was sent off to find herbs and aloe vera for the burns, Faradilla and Xin Hui were sent to the vegetable garden to bring back as many vegetables as they could carry. Vinod, who could climb trees almost as well as a monkey, was sent to gather fruit, and Joseph was to help Yusof dress the burns with aloe vera, and, where they had become infected, with Propolis cream which Yusof had made using propolis from beehives.

"Did you know, propolis is nature's natural anti-biotic? A beehive is more sterile than an operating theatre." Yusof told them.

After that, they would arrange the bedding, food and water.

Some hours later, all the animals were resting, fed and watered. Their bedding was on the ground, in holes and dens, in the trees. Everywhere, there were exhausted animals. Yusof's wife, Aishah, who had helped the children for a while, emerged from the house.

"Come on" she said. "You all need a shower, and then I've made a big jug of lime juice and Nasi Goreng for us all. You are starving, I am sure." Gratefully, they trudged towards the house. None of them had the energy to talk. Aishah took their filthy clothes away to wash and handed each of them a clean sarong and tee shirt.

Xin Hui particularly liked Yusof's house. It was built on stilts with a high, peaked roof, which kept it cool. It was built of hardwood and had attap thatches for the roof. They called the verandah the anjung, and inside there were separate areas for men and for women. Sitting around the dinner table on the anjung, having scrubbed themselves clean and eaten every scrap of food on the table, they gradually began to talk. Each of the children was in a state of shock. They knew the forest was being fired at an alarming rate, but only Ibrahim had experienced it previously. Yusof and Aishah told the children that, as far as they could see, the whole forest was to be torched over time, that in only a few years' there would be no forest left. The palm oil barons were greedy, wanting more and more land for their palm oil trees, and the local palm oil baron was greedier than most.

"But why, why do they want to grow so much palm oil? asked Xin Hui.

"It's used a lot in the Western world." said Yusof. "They put it in cakes, margarine, all sorts of preserved foods, and people eat a lot of preserved foods there. They are also experimenting, trying to make fuels out of it, because petrol is so expensive, and oil from the ground is getting harder and harder to find. It's a lucrative crop. The barons get rich."

"But they can't, they can't burn the forest" cried Vinod. Faradilla was crying, big tears rolling down her face. Xin Hui was angry. She jumped up from the table and paced up and down. Ibrahim sat quietly. He was very worried. He knew more of what his father was telling them than any of the others did, except, perhaps, Faradilla. He put his arm around her.

Joseph, a little older than the others, thought for a while. Then he said, "Let's start a petition. We can do it through our schools, and I know my Mum and Dad will help." He looked up.

It was now dark, and none of them had noticed.

"Well, yes, of course" said Yusof, ever the polite and gentle man. He was not sure what these children or their parents could do, but any help was better than none.

While the children called their parents, Aishah cleared away the dishes, made another couple of jugs of lime juice and put glasses and a bowl of nuts on the table.

Joseph's parents were first to arrive. They were worried; Joseph was out far later than he ever had been previously. Yusof put their minds at ease, explaining quietly that the children were all heroes in a way. Then Vinod's parents and Xin Hui's parents arrived simultaneously. They, too, had been worried about their children. Everyone chattered at once until Yusof clapped his hands.

"Ladies, Gentlemen" he said "You should be very proud of your children, of what they have achieved today. Today, they saved over a hundred animals from the forest fire. They have helped me dress wounds, and feed, water, and bed down the animals, and they have even helped administer ointments and medicines where they were needed."

In his quiet manner, Yusof went on to explain what had happened, his concerns for the forest, how the children had saved the animals, how they had all fought together to try and quench the flames. He explained that the livelihood of many local people depended on the forest, that God really intended us to have a balance with nature, and that if we destroyed the forests, there would be nothing left but concrete, and no forest herbs, medicines, beautiful creatures, to enrich our lives.

Aishah moved softly amongst them, offering lime juice and nuts. She invited everyone to sit down.

Joseph stood up. "I think we should start a 'Save the Forest' campaign" he said. "If we all do it at our schools, use the computers, the internet, then we can perhaps spread it across the world." The parents murmured in approval.

Mr Chan, Xin Hui's father, was the first to speak.

"That is a very good idea," he said, "And it will give Xin Hui a real interest outside school time. We can help her, of course."

Xin Hui interrupted "But the holidays have just started. We won't be going back to school for weeks."

"I'm sure there is still a lot you children can do." said Mr Brown, smiling.

And then Mr Singh chipped in, "And Vinod", he said, "We've always been aware that whilst we're at work, he has so little to do". Mrs Singh agreed, as did Mrs Chan.

Joseph's mother said:"But I don't think we should leave it all to the children. This is a worthy cause, and I, for one, would like to support it as well. I'm sure I can get my lady friends to help."

Mr Brown said:"Darling, you're absolutely right. We should all get involved in this. What does everyone else think?"

There was a chorus of assent. The children jumped up and down in their excitement, forgetting their fatigue. Yusof brushed a tear off his cheek. He was overwhelmed.

"So grateful for your gracious involvement" he said "but I believe the children should take the lead in this. What they have done today is wonderful and amazing, considering their ages." Everyone agreed, and they all started chattering again.

By now it was dark, the crickets were chirping their monotonous song, everyone was sitting on the anjung talking, by candlelight. Ibrahim took a lantern, holding it high, he said "Would you like to see the animals we rescued?" There was a chorus of assent from the grown-ups. He led them towards the bedding areas. Exhausted, in pain, and already settled down for the night, the animals were not nervous as the curious humans peered at them in the half light. They seemed to be aware the humans meant them no harm.

The parents were silent, overwhelmed by what they had seen, what their children had achieved. They had never previously given any thought to the destruction of the forest, the ever-expanding palm oil plantations. It was something they simply lived with. The smoke pall when the forest was burning was a nuisance, but otherwise their lives had not been greatly affected. A lot of people claimed to get respiratory problems and asthma as a result of the smoke pall, but that did not really affect them. Perhaps it needed something like this to happen to make them sit up and think.

Each engrossed in his or her own thoughts, they walked back towards the house.

Mr Brown broke the silence.

"Well, today has been a long day" he said, giving Joseph a quick hug. "I think we should all discuss this at home tomorrow, and take it from there. But if you children really want to do something about the burning of forest land, I, for one, am prepared to do whatever I can to help you."

The other parents agreed. The children, happy at receiving their parents' approval, but exhausted themselves, were falling asleep on their feet. Yusof and Aishah thanked them again, and they all made their way home. Ibrahim and Faradilla fell asleep immediately, curled up on the anjung, Katak between them. Yusof and Aishah decided to leave them where they were. The other children fell asleep in the car. Mr Singh and Mr Chan were able to carry Vinod and Xin Hui into their respective houses, but Mr Brown shook Joseph awake, so that he could walk in to the house.

Ibrahim rescues the baby orang-utan

CHAPTER

The next morning the children all slept late. It did not matter. By time they woke, Mr Singh, Mr and Mrs Chan, and Mr Brown had gone off to work long since. Yusof had gone out as far as he could into the still burning forest, rounding up more waifs and strays, estimating the damage done by the fire. The damage caused was extensive. Many of his precious medicine trees, like the Cinchona, Mahogany, Almacida, Kauri, and many others, had been burned down. The fire had been so ferocious and fast that far more animals than he had originally imagined had been killed, or left near to death, even birds, which would normally have been able to escape.

Of course, like everyone else in Malagiar, the Singhs, the Chans and the Browns had maids who looked after the children in their absence, but, in reality the children had pretty much a free hand as to what they did during the day. They had been firm friends for the past year. It was Ibrahim who had shown them the forest but Joseph, as the oldest, generally took charge. Now, he telephoned Ibrahim.

"Hi, Ibrahim. How's it going?" he asked. "Are the animals O.K.?"

"They're O.K." Ibrahim said. "Bapa's gone out to the forest to see if there are any more which need help. He'll bring them back. Don't worry. But I've got to feed all those here, dress their wounds, and change their bedding. I need help. Will you come?"

"Great!" said Joseph.

It was really what he wanted to hear. It would be great to get truly involved with the animals, like Ibrahim. He admired Ibrahim, envied his knowledge. Joseph had always wanted a dog of his own, but his parents travelled so much, they said it would not be fair to keep one, and Joseph had to agree with them.

"I'll round up Xin Hui and Vinod as well" he said. "We'll all come".

"Allah be praised. Thanks!" said Ibrahim.

An hour later, the little troop arrived at the Kampong. They found Ibrahim and Faradilla already hard at work. Xin Hui joined Faradilla. Under Aishah's supervision, they washed feeding bowls and drinking bowls, filling up the drinking bowls with fresh water, and then the feeding bowls. They removed soiled bedding and added fresh bedding, mostly leaves. They made a big mound of dirty bedding and uneaten food at the edge of the kampong. Aishah told them it would rot and make good compost to feed the crops.

Yusof had already instructed Ibrahim to build more beds, more dens, more safe places for rescued animals. He knew there would be many new arrivals. Ibrahim set Vinod, the tree climber, the task of building platforms as high up as he could in the trees and piling them up with fresh leaves and sweet smelling foliage.

"How many shall I make?" asked Vinod.

CHAPTER 2

"As many as you can, and not too close to each other" said Ibrahim.

Joseph was given the task of sawing up wood to make pens and dens and bird boxes. Ibrahim deftly put them together, tying planks of wood with woven liana strands.

As the day progressed, other villagers arrived, usually carrying some hurt creature, which they had rescued. Some of them stayed to help, some brought food and drinks for the workers. They chatted among themselves as they worked. There was a lot of laughter, and the work went on.

Then Yusof returned. He had with him some little dark men, wiry, sparsely dressed and carrying spears. They looked fierce. Between them, it seemed to the children, they had brought hundreds of animals along, all wounded, hurt, requiring attention.

"Who are those men?" whispered Xin Hui, huddling up to Faradilla.

"They're the Orang Asli" whispered Faradilla. "They live in the forest. That one with the feathers in his headband is the head man. We do not see them very often."

Joseph and Vinod were wide-eyed. They moved closer to the girls. But Ibrahim was quite at home. He went up the head man and, holding his hands together, he bowed. The head man, in turn acknowledged Ibrahim with a solemn bow himself. Yusof patted him on the back.

"Come" he spoke in their own dialect. "Come and let us put these animals to rest, and then you must join us for food".

Yusof issued orders quickly and quietly; everyone was doing something. It appeared chaotic; it seemed the whole village had turned out to help. Nonetheless, animals were quickly getting treated.

Ibrahim had gone off into the jungle with the Orang Asli to collect herbs and medicines, the girls were collecting fruit and vegetables from the garden, Joseph and Vinod were helping Yusof treat the animals. As soon as they were treated, the men of the village took them off to a quiet den, platform, or roost, or whatever they needed, and made sure they had food and drink. The women had been busy helping Aishah and, in no time at all, there was a veritable feast laid out on the padang. The Orang Asli had returned from the forest with Ibrahim, but would not join the others for food. They slipped, unnoticed, back into the forest.

There was a large water butt and a trough full of clean water on the edge of the padang, and everyone washed there before settling down to eat. The women all wore traditional colourful sarongs, and looked very pretty, thought Xin Hui wistfully, with fresh flowers in their hair. The grown-ups were chatting in Malay. Vinod, Xin Hui and Joseph understood a little, but not enough. Ibrahim had to translate for them.

"They're not very happy." he said. "They think the kampong will be taken over by this palm oil chap, and it will be burned down, like the forest. If that happens, we shall all be re-housed in little high rise flats. We shall not be allowed to grow our own food, or keep our animals."

"I would rather die." said Faradilla, emphatically. "I do not want to live in a high-rise, and I want to keep our garden, and our animals. I want to continue living by the jungle. This is my home." She started to cry. The children were all silent.

Then Joseph said "I wonder if we can do anything. Anything to stop this, I mean. You know, the power of numbers?!."

"What can we do?" asked Ibrahim. "We're just five children. Who would take any notice of us?"

"Let me think" said Joseph. "We've got to stop this evil palm oil baron somehow." He was silent.

"Ouch" shouted Vinod.

He had been hit on the head with a persimmon, thrown by one of the young orang utans.

"Hey you. Watch that!" he shouted.

The others laughed. The orang-utan grinned, and raised his hand to throw another persimmon, but this time Vinod ducked and it missed. Just then, a macaque jumped up in front of him, and stole his banana. Vinod snatched at it, but it was a futile effort.

"Hee, hee, hee" shouted the orang utan, jumping gleefully up and down on its perch.

"He is so naughty" giggled Xin Hui.

"Yes" said Ibrahim seriously, "but I shall have to talk to his father. The people here will not like it if he throws things at them."

"Can you really talk to the animals?" asked Vinod, whose approach to life was purely scientific.

"Well, yes, I suppose so" said Ibrahim. "At least, I talk to them and they understand me, and I understand what they are saying."

"Come on, then. Let's go and talk to him now" said the disbelieving Vinod.

Ibrahim shrugged. He knew that Vinod thought he was a crackpot. He got up, and the children followed him to where the orang-utan family were settling down for the night.

"Tunku" he called.

CHAPTER 2

"What! You call him Tunku!" said Vinod, incredulous.

"Yes, that's his name", said Ibrahim, and his wife is called Puteri".

"But even I know that means Prince and Princess".

"So! They are a prince and a princess in the orang-utan kingdom. They are the heads of their clan. If you treat them with respect, they will respond."

'Ibrahim can be so awesome!' thought Joseph.

Faradilla, smiling, pulled at Ibrahim's sleeve. With her thumb she indicated, further up the tree, Puteri, waving her hand and grinning from ear to ear.

"Tunku" Ibrahim continued, smiling too. "Your baby is doing well, making good progress. You will be reunited with him in just a few days. But I need you to tell your number one son that it is not a good idea to throw missiles at these people who are trying to help you. I do not want him to make them angry, so that they stop helping."

He bowed.

Tunku bowed in return. Vinod's mouth dropped open. Tunku grunted, then, grunting, he climbed higher up into the tree.

"What did he say?" asked Joseph, wholly in awe of what he had seen.

"He said it's fine. The youngster will be taken firmly under control. Not to worry." said Ibrahim.

"But how? How do you do it?" demanded Vinod.

"I do not know." said Ibrahim. "It just happens."

"Can you understand all the animals?"

"Most of them."

"Wow." Vinod was convinced at last.

Xin Hui thought that when she grew up, she might marry Ibrahim. He was so clever. But, on the other hand, her parents wanted her to marry a doctor or a solicitor, so perhaps she might not.

Joseph was more determined than ever that they MUST do something to help these animals, these people, this jungle, this forest. *'Just one fat money-grabbing evil palm oil baron is not going to get the better of us'* he thought.

He was distracted by little Faradilla. She had a small civet cat in her arms. She was cooing at it gently, making soft noises, and the civet cat was watching her, head cocked on one side, purring.

"Can you talk to the animals too?" asked Joseph.

"Not as well as Ibrahim" she answered, as she limped off.

Her little figure limping off into the night made Joseph feel protective. She had fallen when very young, they all knew, and broken her leg. It had not set properly, and she would limp for the rest of her life. 'She's only six' thought Joseph who, at thirteen, felt very grown up.

The villagers were wending their way back to their own homes. Yusof called the children to help him check the animals finally before retiring for the night. It had been a long day, he was tired. Aishah cleared away the remainder of the dishes from the padang, taking them to the kitchen to be washed and put away.

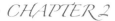
Joseph called a taxi. At thirteen, the eldest, he took charge of Xin Hui and Vinod, dropping them off at their respective homes on the way back.

Mr and Mrs Brown were in the drawing room, having a gin and tonic, discussing the news they had just watched on television. Joseph burst in.

"Mum! Dad! I've got this great idea. You know that uncle Yusof is worried the evil palm oil baron is going to burn down all the forest, and their kampong too. What do you think, why don't I e.mail all my friends, get a campaign going to save the forest? I can get the school involved. I'm sure Miss Thompson will help. Will you help too? Then I'll e.mail Eric in England, and Helle in Denmark, and ...."

"Hold on, Son" said Mr Brown. "I know how much you're involved in this, but do you know what you're taking on? I'm afraid you'll be disappointed. These oil barons are powerful men, not to be stopped by a small gang of school children."

"But if we can spread it around the world, Dad, we won't be a small gang of school children. We'll be world-wide."

"Well, I take your point. Sleep on it, Son. Now off to bed with you." Mr Brown picked up his gin and tonic and turned to Mrs Brown. She smiled at Joseph.

"Night night, Darling" she said, before resuming her conversation with her husband.

Joseph could not sleep that night. It was hot. He lay, arms behind his head, thinking, day dreaming, working out what they could do. He would get the others together in the morning, tell them his plans. He was sure they'd be pleased, want to join in. He was determined. They would save the jungle – and the kampong. They might only be children, but they could do it. He fell asleep.

CHAPTER 3

The next morning Joseph got up earlier than usual. He was very excited. He rounded up Xin Hui and Vinod, and they set off on their bicycles for the Kampong. They arrived before breakfast. Yusof was surprised to see them so early, and Ibrahim and Faradilla were delighted. Aishah gave them Roti Prata for breakfast, and then they set to work.

Joseph was bursting to tell them of his plan, but they were all too busy feeding animals, cleaning pens and bedding, dressing wounds. It would just have to wait! Wounded, burned animals were still being brought in, but fewer now, and a routine was developing. First they cleaned, then they put in clean food and water, then wounds were attended.

Overall, Yusof was pleased. Most of the creatures were recovering nicely and could soon be released, as were several birds, butterflies and insects. The macaques were recovering well. Some of them had been merely shocked or dazed. Most of the snakes were recovering, although a couple gave cause for concern. The monitor lizard, still in great pain, definitely gave cause for concern. Even if he recovered, it was doubtful whether he would ever be able to fend for himself in the forest again.

Several more slow loris had been brought in since the first day. Unable to move quickly, they had all been badly burned, and were clearly in considerable pain. Some civet cats were still in a state of shock, as were some of the gibbons, and monkeys, but, by and large, Yusof was very satisfied. Virtually all of these animals would survive. The baby orang-utan, while still critical, was over the worst. Yusof had bandaged its hands and feet and covered its back with aloe vera, which would sooth and heal the burns. It's mother would soon be able to nurse it again, which would contribute more than anything else towards its recovery.

At last, the chores were finished. The children sat around on the anjung of Yusof's house. Joseph genuinely thought that if one more thing were asked of him, he would be unable to do it, he would be unable to move. Every joint in his body ached, and he had never felt so tired. They slept, there, on the anjung, for an hour. Aishah woke them eventually.

"You will not sleep tonight if I let you sleep on." she said. "I've made you tea and cake".

The children ate gratefully, and felt refreshed.

"Now" said Joseph "I must tell you my plan. I've been wanting to tell you all day. I think it is a good plan. How many friends have you got, all of you? How many friends can you contact by e.mail? Think about it. Think carefully. Faradilla, you don't have to worry about the e.mail thing".

The children thought, Xin Hui scratching figures in the dust, Vinod staring up at the sky above him, and Ibrahim counting on his fingers.

"Ten" said Xin Hui.

"Sixteen" said Vinod.

"Fourteen" said Ibrahim.

"I've got four friends" said Faradilla, holding up four fingers.

"And I've got fifteen friends here, and twelve cousins in Europe" said Joseph. "That makes"... he did a quick sum ... "seventy-one friends and relatives."

"Oh, we've got relatives too" chorused the others.

"But you did not ask about those" said Vinod.

"Well, let's count relatives too".

The children worked out that, between them they had a hundred and twenty-one friends and relatives they could contact by e.mail.

"Now, what we've got to do, is write an e.mail which we can send to everyone, and they can pass on to their friends and relatives who, in turn, can pass it on to their friends and relatives, and so on. That way, our e.mail will reach hundreds and hundreds of people in no time at all".

Joseph was pleased with himself. This was a great idea. The others sat in silence. Eventually Vinod asked

"What will we say in the e.mail?"

"Well, we've got to tell them what's happening here, about the evil palm oil baron, and how he's destroying the forest, killing and causing suffering to animals, how he's about to take over the kampong." Joseph said.

"We had better start writing the e.mail, lah." said Xin Hui, practical as ever. "What are we going to say?"

"I shall get some pencils and paper" said Ibrahim, going into the house. He emerged, clutching five pencils and sheaves of paper, which he distributed fairly evenly.

"Faradilla, you just sit and listen" he said, "or do a nice drawing for us."

Ibrahim sucked his pencil.

"How do we start?" he asked.

"With the fire" said Xin Hui "That is what started all this."

"O.K." said Vinod. *"Last week, the palm oil baron set fire to the forest"* he wrote laboriously as he spoke.

"No. The evil palm oil baron set fire to the forest, killing or maiming all the animals" said Ibrahim.

"O.K. *"Last week, the evil palm oil baron set fire to the forest, killing or maiming all the animals"* wrote Vinod.

"Cannot!" said Xin Hui "We must explain more, lah. This would not mean anything to my cousins in Shanghai."

"Umm" said Joseph. "My Dad says the world is being taken over by crops like palm oil. And they're not being grown for food, but for bio-fuels. That's where the money is. So, gradually, we're all going to starve because there won't be enough land left to grow food. And" he paused "they're burning the forests too because they're greedy; they say it's because we need more land to grow food. But we all know it's only to plant more palm oil. It's happening all over Asia Dad says".

"You mean it is not just here?" asked Ibrahim.

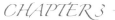

CHAPTER 3

"No" said Joseph. "From what Dad says, it's happening everywhere."

"Well" said Ibrahim. "Vinod, write this down *'Help us save the forests of the world. Here in Malagiar, the evil palm oil baron is burning down the forest – miles and miles of forest. He is killing the medicine trees and shrubs. He is killing or wounding most horribly all the animals. He might even burn down our villages.'* He stopped for breath.

"That's good, Ibrahim" said Joseph. "Did you get it all, Vinod?"

Tongue sticking out, and concentrating hard, Vinod was still writing.

"There!" he said eventually, sitting up. I got it all.

"We can leave that just as it is" said Joseph. "But then we've got to ask for help. What sort of help do we want? In fact, we should put a big heading on it, saying *'We Need Your Help!'*

Vinod wrote at the top of the paper *'We Need Your Help!'*

The children thought for a while. Then Xin Hui said "Remember what you said, Joseph. We have got to spread the word to all the children in the world. But even if we send out lots of e.mails, that is still not doing anything to help us. So – they know what's happening here. What can they do? What can we do about it?"

They all thought.

"What about this?" said Joseph. "We've got to get them to tell everyone what is happening; tell their parents, their friends, their schools, everyone they meet. If we ask them to send e.mails back to us in support, we can forward all those e.mails on to the evil palm oil baron. That's it, when they get our e.mails, they've got to write e.mails back to us condemning the actions of the evil palm oil baron, and we will forward them on."

"Whew!" said Vinod, wiping his brow.

"'We need your help. Forward this e.mail to all your friends, your relatives, your schools. It is very important that you all send an e.mail back to us, and everyone else does too, condemning the actions of the evil palm oil baron. We will forward your e.mails to the palm oil baron himself.' How does that sound?"

"No! No!" said Xin Hui. "If we get very many e.mails, our parents will stop us from using the computers."

"You're right." Joseph frowned. "I've got it" he said suddenly, looking up. "We'll have to get the evil palm oil baron's e.mail address, and get everyone to send protest e.mails to him direct. I'll have a look at his website this evening. The e.mail address is bound to be there."

Ibrahim and Xin Hui clapped their hands, Vinod grinned, chewing on his pencil, and Faradilla smiled happily.

"That's just great!" said Joseph. "I think that's it. Now we've got to change the wording of this e.mail and we must all copy it down, so that we can start sending it out tonight."

The next thirty minutes were quiet as the children wrote, concentrating hard in case they made a mistake:

'Help us save the forests of the world.

Here in Malagiar, the evil palm oil baron is burning down the forest – miles and miles of forest. He is killing the medicine trees and shrubs. He is killing or wounding most horribly all the animals. He even wants to burn down our villages.

CHAPTER 3

We need your help. Forward this e.mail to all your friends, your relatives, your schools. It is very important that you all send an e.mail to the evil palm oil baron, and everyone else does too, condemning what he is doing to the forest and the kampongs. We all have to ask him to stop. His e.mail address is ....'

"We shall have to fill in the e.mail address later."

"But we don't go back to school for another four weeks". Ibrahim said.

"We can still send lots of e.mails before we go back to school." said Joseph.

That evening, all the children were at home early.

Mr and Mrs Chan found Xin Hui working hard at the computer when they, themselves, got home.

"Mummee! Daddee! Look, I'm e.mailing all my friends, and my cousins in Shanghai, telling them all about the evil palm oil baron and how he is burning down the forest."

She knew better than to tell them the plan was for everyone to send e.mails to the evil palm oil baron direct. Mr and Mrs Chan would be worried for their daughter. They did not want her to get into trouble and, instinctively, Xin Hui knew that there could, indeed, be trouble. Mr and Mrs Chan smiled happily. They had a lot of respect for Yusof and Aishah, and were glad their daughter was spending her holiday fruitfully, helping them tend sick animals. It would teach her about compassion.

"Come and eat now" said Mrs Chan. "We're having chicken rice with kailan in oyster sauce. You like that."

"You know what, Mummee, aunty Aishah kills her own chickens when she needs them. She says a prayer and slits

their throats with a big knife, very quickly, lah, and then the blood pours out into a big bowl. They don't feel anything. Joseph says that in England, they wring their necks, or they just chop their heads off. When they do that, the chickens run round the field without their heads for a few minutes."

Mrs Chan winced. She enjoyed eating chicken, but she did not want to know the details of how it was killed.

Mr and Mrs Singh were looking forward to relaxing with the family over a curry dinner that evening. Vinod was waiting for them when they got home, having laid the table and set up as much as he could. Mrs Singh was pleasantly surprised.

"Why, Vinod. How helpful you are." She said.

Mr Singh was washing himself, prior to eating.

"A good Sikh is always a gentleman." he said. "I am glad to see, Vinod, that you are helping your mother."

"Papa, can I please use the computer later? I want to e.mail my cousins and my friends to tell them what we are doing at the kampong."

"I don't see that it can do any harm" said Mr Singh. "After we have prayed and eaten, you may use the computer. But, meantime, we have something to tell you."

Vinod was curious. "What is it, Papa?"

"I think your mother had better tell you, Vinod."

"Mama?"

"Vinod, how would you like a new baby brother or sister?"

"Does that mean I am going to have one?"

"Yes, it does, my son."

"That is very nice" said Vinod, far more interested in getting his e.mails off. He was scarcely able to suppress his delight that his father had given him permission to use the computer.

"Thank you, Papa." He headed off towards the study. Mr and Mrs Singh looked at each other and smiled. They need not have worried that Vinod might be upset at the addition of a new baby to the family.

Joseph had already sent all his e.mails when Mr and Mrs Brown got home. He did tell them what he had done, however, and they were quite happy. He did not tell them about the request for a reply to be sent to the evil palm oil baron. He felt that was best left unsaid.

Mr and Mrs Brown knew Joseph to be a sensible and responsible boy, so they had no concern.

"How is Yusof getting on down there at the kampong?" asked Mr Brown.

"He's got more and more animals coming in. I think he may run out of food and stuff soon. He looks a bit worried." said Joseph. "I haven't said anything to Ibrahim, though' because I know he already worries about his Mum and Dad, and about Faradilla. She's not very strong, you know."

"Maybe I should go and have a word with Yusof tomorrow." Mr Brown said.

Joseph was pleased. He knew he could rely on Dad to sort things out.

CHAPTER 3

Yusof and Aishah sat on the verandah in the cool of the evening. They were both very tired. Faradilla was curled up on a mat in the corner, fast asleep beside Katak. Ibrahim fetched his parents a jug of iced lemon tea. They had already eaten – not much, but enough. Most of the food in the garden had been used in feeding the animals. The herbs and ointments were running out. Yusof's income was meagre. They generally lived well, but only because their lifestyle was modest and Aishah was able to supplement his income by selling surplus fruit, vegetables, rice, and eggs. And now there was no surplus left.

"Ayah, may I use the computer?" Ibrahim asked.

"Yes, Ibrahim, you may." answered his father. "Don't worry, my wife, tomorrow is another day. And Allah willing, we shall survive."

Ibrahim, too, sent off his e.mails. All they had to do now, he thought, was wait. He decided that, the next day, after they had fed and watered the animals, he would go down to the burned forest. None of the children had been back since the fire. He wanted to see what it looked like now.

CHAPTER 4

The next day Ibrahim told Joseph of his plan to return to the burned part of the forest – just to have a look! Vinod, Xin Hui and Faradilla refused to be left out and so, after a light lunch, they set off, on their bicycles this time. Tunku, the orang-utan, had insisted on going with them. Ibrahim pedaled along with Tunku perched precariously on the crossbar, his long coat of fine red hair hanging down like a curtain. Tunku was so big, Ibrahim could not see around him, and had to cycle with his head peering out from around the side of the great ape. It was not an easy journey. But Tunku was determined. He had one long arm wrapped around the handlebars and the other wrapped firmly around Ibrahim's neck. He was at least four times bigger than Ibrahim, and furry too. He made Ibrahim feel very hot and uncomfortable, but Ibrahim was far too polite to ask him to get off.

When they arrived at the still smouldering forest, the children were dismayed. Tunku actually cried. There was nothing left except burned stubble, blackened tree stumps turned to charcoal, and ash. Everywhere, there was ash. The ground was still hot and smoking.

"Quick" whispered Faradilla "Hide. I hear voices."

Faradilla's hearing was acute. The children did not question her. They hid their bikes quickly behind a large tree. There was a hollow in the ground a few feet away, still grassy. The children dove into it. Tunku squeezed in too. They pulled some small branches over themselves, so that they were well hidden.

"Why are we hiding?" asked Xin Hui.

"Quiet" whispered Joseph. "If Faradilla heard someone coming, it might be the evil palm oil baron's men."

Tunku fidgeted and grunted.

"Tunku, we think the evil men are coming" whispered Ibrahim. "We must not let them find us here. We have to be very quiet and still."

Tunku grunted again, softly, and remained as still and quiet as the others. They watched as several men approached along the dirt road. They wore loose trousers tucked into working boots, some had no shirts on, and they all wore yellow helmets like those worn at building sites. They were well-muscled, dark, and sunburned. As they walked, they kicked up the dust, which rose in small swirls behind them.

The children did not dare move. They could now hear what the men were saying

"Well, the ground's still too hot, so we'll have to wait. Unless, of course, it rains in the meantime" said one. "I'll tell you what we'll do. We'll wait a week, and then start."

Another man interrupted.

"We can't start next week, boss, the tractors are all out, and we need the diggers too. They're out at Kulamintang right now, digging up the earth there. They'll be back in two weeks' time. From what I see" he said, looking around "you'll be lucky if the ground's cool enough to start in less than two weeks."

The first man sighed.

"You're right. Two weeks it is. But because of the delay, we'll have to fire the rest of the forest at the same time."

The children looked at each other.

"Fire the rest of the forest?" mouthed Vinod to Joseph.

"The boss says we need at least another two hundred hectares."

The men walked on, their boots crunching the dry ground underfoot, still kicking up the dust. The children stayed where they were. They did not dare move for another five minutes. Then they exploded from their hiding place, all talking at once.

"At least another two hundred hectares!"

"We can't let them."

"We've got to stop them."

"We've got two weeks!"

"What can we do?" – the practical Xin Hui again!

Tunku knew the children were agitated, but he did not understand them.

"Hooh, Hooh" he grunted, pushing Ibrahim gently but firmly, in the stomach.

"Tunku" said Ibrahim "they are going to burn a lot more forest. They have not finished yet."

The children sat on the ground, silent, overwhelmed by what they had just heard.

"We must be able to do something, lah" said Xin Hui half-heartedly, chewing on a piece of grass.

"I think we should go and tell Bapa" Ibrahim said.

Crestfallen, they trudged back to the kampong, pushing their bikes. None of them felt like pedaling. Tunku trudged along with them, fists trailing on the ground, head resting on his chest. He was very depressed.

When they got to the kampong, Yusof and Aishah were not there. The children were unaware that they were having a meeting in the coffee shop up the road with Mr Brown.

Tunku climbed up into a tree where Puteri was waiting for him. Clearly he communicated what was happening because, gradually, all the apes, monkeys, and birds started making a noise which built up into an excited crescendo of sound.

While they waited, the children talked.

"Bapa says fire breaks stop forest fires."

"What are firebreaks?"

"Well. They're sort of like a road or wide ditch which is cleared through the forest. It has to be wide enough so that the fire can't jump across it. Then, if there is a fire, it can only burn so far before it is stopped."

"We can dig a firebreak" shouted Vinod happily.

He jumped up.

"That is what we can do. We can dig a firebreak."

"We can't do it on our own" said Joseph. "It would have to be miles long. And we've only got two weeks."

Joseph thought.

"Maybe" he said "we could do it if we had help. Ibrahim, would the village people help? And what about the Orang-Asli? It's more their forest than anyone else's."

"I think they might" said Ibrahim, eyes gleaming now.

"We need as much help as we can get. We can all ask the parents to bring their friends along to help, and perhaps I can ask the priest at Church to say something to the congregation" Joseph was thinking out loud.

"And I can ask the priest at the Hindu temple, and the Granthi at the Gurdwara" said Vinod gravely.

"Perhaps I can ask the monks" said Xin Hui.

"And I can ask the Imam" said Ibrahim

"Would you come with me. I am a bit scared to go on my own" said Vinod.

"Me, too" said Xin Hui.

The children agreed that they would all go together to ask the Imam, the Buddhist monks, the Sikh granthi, and the Catholic and Hindu priests to help them save the forest from the evil palm oil baron. They would go that very evening.

"I want to talk to Tunku. I have an idea." Ibrahim was smiling broadly. He winked at Joseph as he walked towards Tunku's tree.

CHAPTER 4

He climbed up the tree, onto Tunku's platform. The others could see him squatting there, talking to Tunku and Puteri. Ibrahim sat quietly. Tunku and Puteri were hooting and grunting, gesticulating excitedly. Occasionally Tunku would grab a branch and shake it furiously. Many of the other apes and monkeys had gathered around to listen. They were getting excited too. The children below wondered what was going on.

Ibrahim climbed down.

"I think we can do it." he said.

"What?"

"How?"

"When?" the children asked simultaneously.

"We should ask the grown-ups. Ask what they think." said Xin Hui, fearful that she was getting into something naughty. She was anxious not to upset her parents.

"When Bapa returns, we should talk to him first" said Ibrahim. "I am thirsty. Does anyone else want a drink?" He disappeared into the kitchen, and returned carrying a tray with five glasses and a jug of water.

Faradilla had the burned civet cat on her lap. It was rapidly becoming a pet, but she knew that Yusof would not allow that. He insisted that all the forest animals had to be returned to the wild as soon as they were better.

"They are not domestic animals" he explained. "They would die of broken hearts if we kept them here. They are designed to be free. Cats and dogs, however, are designed to be domestic pets."

The children drank thirstily.

"Don't forget, we've got to check our e.mails this evening" said Joseph.

"Ooh, I'd forgotten. So much excitement, lah!" said Xin Hui. She was looking forward to hearing from her friends, and especially her cousins in Shanghai.

They were all looking forward to checking their e.mails that evening.

"Now." Ibrahim said, scarcely able to contain himself. "Do you want to know what Tunku said?"

Having deliberately delayed the telling of it, he now could not bear to wait any longer.

"Yes. Yes" they chorused.

"Tunku says he is going to call a Grand Conference with all the animals in the forest. He's going to call in the elephants and the rhinoceros. He's going to call in the bears, the cats and the snakes, and all the animals who can dig. He's going to call in the apes, the monkeys, the birds, the bats, the lizards, the anteaters, the porcupines. He will leave nobody out. He's already started to spread the word. By tomorrow morning, everyone in the forest will know about it."

The children were amazed. The clamour in the treetops was now a deafening roar. In the treetops, they could see all the creatures rushing about, swooping, swinging, gliding. The undergrowth was rustling, bristling with movement. Excitement was in the air.

"Can he do that? Can he really do that?" asked Vinod, incredulous.

Ibrahim smiled quietly.

"You must have faith in the animals, Vinod" he said.

"When are they having the conference?"

"Can we go too?"

"But what are they going to do?" asked Xin Hui.

"Tunku thinks that, if he can persuade them, they will help us build a firebreak through the forest, so that the evil palm oil baron's men cannot burn down any more."

"They'll be able to burn down a little" said Joseph thoughtfully. "We'll have to dig the firebreak about fifty feet back from the road at the edge of the forest. The evil palm oil baron's men must not see it. I think they will start firing the forest at the edge, where it has already burned out. It's easier that way. If the fire break is a few feet back, where they cannot see it, it will be safe. If they see it, they will fill it in, and they will be angry too. It's best that they do not know."

Ibrahim was impressed.

"How do you know all that?" he asked.

"Oh, my Dad told me about firebreaks when we were in Sabah."

"When are they having the conference?" Vinod asked, again.

"As soon as possible" said Ibrahim. "There is no time to waste."

Just then, Yusof and Aishah returned.

"Ayah, Ibu" called Ibrahim, "we have so much to tell you."

"We have something to tell you, too" said Yusof.

He climbed on to the anjung.

"Now, children, gather round" he said. Yusof was beaming. All the children were aware that, recently, his brow had been furrowed with worry. This new, smiling Yusof was strange to them.

"Mr Brown has just visited us, and he has been very kind. From his workmates, he has raised $5,000 for us, to help pay for the food and medicines for the animals. He has also suggested that we start a charity. He would be happy to be on the Board, and the charity would be to protect and preserve the forest, the plants, the animals, especially including" he said, beaming, "the medicinal plants. It would make all we are doing here both legitimate and of public interest, so that funds will be raised to help us. I believe it is a very good idea, but I would like your opinions. You children have been, after all, instrumental in getting everything we are doing here started."

Aishah joined them. She, too, was happy. They now had money to fund the feeding and welfare of the animals, to plant and succour seedlings, especially those of the rare medicinal plants, and, generally, to preserve the forest as best they could. She could hardly believe it. It was all too much to take in.

"Ayah, that's wonderful!"

Ibrahim spoke for them all. Faradilla gave her father a big hug, and then her mother. Vinod, Xin Hui and Joseph smiled happily. This was wonderful news. Xin Hui gave Yusof a kiss on the cheek, and then Aishah. Vinod, sheepishly, shook Yusof's hand, and then Aishah's. Joseph shook both their hands. Ibrahim waited until last, but then he hugged his mother hard, and threw himself at his father, giving him the tightest hug he could.

CHAPTER 4

"Now, Ayah, Ibu, we have news too" he announced.

"We went back to the forest today, to where the fire was. We saw the evil palm oil baron's men, and we heard them talking. They are going to fire another two hundred hectares. They are going to do it in two weeks' time. And we have talked to Tunku, and....."

"Steady, steady" said Yusof. "Are you absolutely sure of this?"

"Yes, absolutely" chorused the children.

"And, anyway" Ibrahim continued "we can dig a firebreak. If the villagers and the Orang Asli help. And Tunku's calling a conference with all the creatures of the forest, and he will ask them to help as well. He says they will because they are fed up with the burning, and they want to preserve the forest. And the parents will help, and we are going to ask the Imam, the monks, and the priests..."

"Hold on" said Yusof. "Are you telling me that you intend digging a firebreak, in two weeks?"

"Yes, yes, but only if the villagers and the Orang Asli, everyone else, and the animals will help us. We cannot do it on our own, of course."

"I will have to speak to Mr Brown about this" said Yusof, "but it sounds like a plan which might work. I am sure the parents and the villagers will help, and the Orang Asli are very anxious about the preservation of their life style. As for Tunku; you, Ibrahim, know him better than any of us. If you believe he can do it, all the better. With the animals of the forest on our side, it gives us very great strength."

"Can you speak to the villagers and the Orang Asli, Yusof?" asked Joseph.

"I will speak to them." Yusof got up. "I must now tend the animals. But" he said, smiling, "we have all had good news today, and I feel greatly heartened."

"We'll come and help" called Ibrahim, and the children followed him down to what they now called the animal kampong. It was overflowing with animals. Every square foot was taken up with sick, burned, wounded, or shocked creatures. They were continuously being brought in, and Yusof did not have the heart to turn them away. Some of the animals were too badly hurt ever to be returned to the forest. In time, he would have to create a permanent home for them where they would be looked after for the rest of their lives, but that was something to think about later. There was enough to occupy him right now.

CHAPTER 5

The evil palm oil baron's company was called Universal Palm Oil Inc. He had built splendid offices for himself. A long drive through the palm oil plantation opened up on to a big space with grassy green lawns, flowerbeds where gladioli and heliconia grew alongside bird of paradise, and bougainvillea and frangipani trees. There was a big lake in front of the building with fountains tossing gallons of cool water into the air, sparkling and dancing in the sunlight.

The building itself, built of glass and chrome, sparkled as if encrusted with diamonds. There was a huge entrance foyer, all marble and glass, with glass lifts going up as if into the sky. The evil palm oil baron's office was on the top floor. He had a huge penthouse suite. The walls were sheer glass, and, from there, he could look out for miles and miles over his estates. He had a big rosewood desk in the middle of the room, and a fat, squidgy leather chair behind it. A dish of nuts and another of Turkish delight were on the desk, a crystal glass with amber liquid in it, a couple of files, and a big glass ashtray. A thick Bedouin rug was on the marble floor, and beautiful pictures on the walls. A cocktail cabinet and a filing cabinet were in a corner. Beyond his desk, the evil palm oil baron had placed a comfortable low sofa and coffee table. A crystal chandelier hung from the ceiling. Lavish and opulent as his office was, the evil palm oil baron, at this particular moment, appeared to derive no pleasure from it.

He was short and squat. His thick neck was like a bull's. He wore an expensive designer label suit, but it sat uncomfortably on his square frame. Shirt collar unbuttoned, he pulled angrily at his tie. He was sweating, damp, greasy hair slicked back. Cold, black eyes slit against the smoke from the cigar he held in his hand, he was pacing back and forth across the office, shouting at the skinny manager who cringed, head bowed, hands together, just in front of the door, desperate to escape the onslaught of the evil palm oil baron's diatribe.

"Are you telling me" shouted the evil palm oil baron "that our systems are clogged up with e.mails?"

"Y yes, Sir" stammered the skinny manager.

"These e.mails are from children? Mere children? You can't do anything about it, stop them?"

Agitated, he was gesticulating frantically with his cigar, waving it about as he shouted. His fat face was red and sweating, getting redder and redder. The evil palm oil baron was accustomed to getting his own way. He had managed to bribe or bully his way through most adversities, but this was different.

"Pay them off!" he shouted.

"S Sir" whispered the terrified skinny manager, "there are too many of them. We have received over five thousand e.mails in the last couple of days, and they just keep coming."

CHAPTER 5

"Block them. Block them" screamed the evil palm oil baron.

"Forgive me, Sir, but we cannot do that. If we block these e.mails, we will block all e.mails coming in. The business will shut down." whispered the still terrified skinny manager.

"They're telling us not to burn the forest, not to plant palm oil? The monsters! Who do they think they are? I hate children. I will not be dictated to by them. I will not allow it. They know nothing!" he screamed.

The skinny manager plucked up a little courage

"Sir" he suggested "it might be a good idea to sit down".

He was worried the evil palm oil baron might have a heart attack. He was very red in the face and breathing heavily. He was sweating so much that, despite the air conditioning, his shirt was soaked, and little rivulets of sweat were running down his face and neck. He drew heavily on his cigar.

Encouraged, the skinny manager continued

"As it is, the system is getting so clogged up with these e.mails that it cannot cope. Everything is scrambled."

"Sort it out!" screamed the evil palm oil baron "That's what I pay you for. Sort it out. Go!"

"Yes sir"

Turning, the skinny manager hurtled through the door as fast as he could, glad to be out of the evil palm oil baron's office. Out of his sight! He did not know what to do. The computer systems were seizing up. The computer manager was doing his best, but could not cope. And HE was having to take all the flack. Life was so unfair!

CHAPTER 5

The evil palm oil baron slumped down in the chair behind his desk. He mopped his brow. He reached for the glass of whisky already poured, and drank it down in one gulp. He felt a little calmer.

That stupid manager would have to sort things out. That was what he was paid for. And WHY was he letting a bunch of children upset him so much? Once the problem had been resolved he, the great palm oil baron, would sack him. But he would let him resolve the problem first. He sat for a while, in silence. He calmed down enough to start thinking. *'That's it. That's what I shall do.'* he thought.

'Now let's get back to making money. Lovely money, here I come'. He rubbed his hands. His overseer would arrive for a meeting in five minutes. He would take the time to calm himself a little more, then he would arrange for five hundred thousand more hectares of forest to be burned down – not two hundred. He laughed. 'And what will those silly children be able to do about it? Nothing!'

By the time the overseer arrived, the evil palm oil baron was in a better frame of mind. He was delighted at his own cleverness. Those children would not possibly believe that he might burn down five hundred thousand hectares of forest all at once. He would teach them not to criticize, not to interfere. He giggled to himself. His whole body shook with the effort.

The overseer listened in silence as the evil palm oil baron explained what was required. A hardened man, he had worked for the evil palm oil baron for a long time. He nodded. He knew what to do.

"I want five hundred thousand hectares razed to the ground, not two hundred. Do you hear? Razed to the ground! And you are to start tomorrow. I want no delay; nothing is to stop you." shouted the evil palm oil baron, working himself up into a terrible temper again as he thought of the audacity of the children sending him e.mails from all over the world.

"But, Sir, we cannot, lah. The diggers, the caterpillars, all the other equipment is still at Kulamintang, The men have got to finish that job, and then bring the equipment down to the forest here. However hard they work, it will be two weeks before we can start." He was a practical man.

The evil palm oil baron cried out in frustration. He waved his arms about, burning himself on the wrist with the stub of his cigar. "Ouch! Aiyee!" he yelled.

The overseer grabbed the jug of water from the desk and threw it over the evil palm oil baron's burned wrist. Water dripped on to the floor. Angrily stomping about, the evil palm oil baron slipped on the wet marble, falling, and banging his head against the rosewood desk as he fell. Making a strange noise like air escaping from a balloon, he slithered down the side of the desk. He had knocked himself out. Moreover, he had a big gash in his head, which was bleeding. The overseer might have been a practical man, but he was terrified at the consequences of what he had done. HE had thrown water over the evil palm oil baron's wrist, making him slip and fall. He panicked. The evil palm oil baron lay on the ground bleeding. The overseer rushed backwards and forwards across the office, wondering what to do. Then, after a few seconds, he went in search of the skinny office manager. The skinny office manager found the first aid officer, and they all crept gingerly into the evil palm oil baron's office. He was still in a huddle on the floor. The first aid officer cleaned and dressed his head wound with a big pink plaster. They called in a couple of office clerks to help them and, between them, they lifted the evil palm oil baron into his armchair. After a few minutes the evil palm oil baron started to come round. He groaned. The skinny office manager was anxiously wringing his hands – a bad habit! The overseer was scared, and the first aid officer waited close to the door so that he could escape as soon as possible. The evil palm oil baron opened his eyes, he took in the three of them standing there, and then he roared. He roared and roared.

"Get those dratted children" he roared.

"Yes, sir" they chorused, all at once, falling over themselves to get out of the office. The evil palm oil baron clutched his head, which was hurting. He rocked back and forth in his chair. He felt very sorry for himself.

"Why is all this happening to me. I do not deserve this." he moaned as he rocked back and forth, head in hands. "Those children are to blame for this."

CHAPTER

Puteri was anxious. Tunku had been gone for nine hours, and it was now dusk. It would be dark within minutes. He should be back by now. Anything could have happened to him. His mission had been fraught with danger. Not all the animals in the forest were friendly. Not all the indigenous people were friendly either. He could have been attacked, injured, killed even! She climbed up higher into the tree, as high as she could, so that she could see as much of the forest as possible. Perhaps she might spot him making his way back. Nothing!

From high up there, she watched Yusof and Ibrahim doing the rounds of the animal pens and cages, the holes in the ground and the platforms in the trees. Methodically, slowly, they checked all the animals, ensured they were safe, comfortable, and settled for the night ahead. But the animals were not settled this evening. A storm was coming. They could feel it. Lightning was flashing through the sky. They were restless, waiting for Tunku's return, waiting for the rain. They, too, were worried, wondering what had become of Tunku. Angrily, Puteri shook the branches.

CHAPTER 6

"Hooh, Hooh, Hooh!" she called, hoping Tunku might hear her. But there was no answering call. The wind was blowing strongly now, bending the trees. Black clouds were billowing in, fast and furious. Puteri climbed down to the platform where Yusof had slung her baby in a small hammock. Scooping the frightened baby out of the hammock, she cradled it in her arms as she climbed into the nest she had built out of branches and leaves on the platform. When the rain came, she would at least keep her baby dry. She would not sleep until Tunku returned.

"Hurry, Ibrahim" urged Yusof. "The rain will come any minute. There's nothing more we can do here. It's the storm which is unsettling the animals. Let's get back to the house."

Just as he spoke, the first big drops of rain came. There was lightning, followed by an enormous clap of thunder. They ran towards the house where Aishah and Faradilla were waiting for them. Just as they reached the anjung, the heavens opened. The rain came down in great driving sheets, lightning cracked overhead, the thunder rolled on and on. Every other sound was drowned out by the howling wind, the roar of the falling rain and the rolling thunder.

"Tunku's still not back, Ayah" shouted Ibrahim.

"He will be alright" Yusof shouted back "He is well respected in the forest. He can look after himself."

The rain was driving in, on to the anjung. They went into the house. That evening, they ate indoors.

Deep in the forest, Tunku took shelter under the branches of a wide-leafed tree. It had taken him longer than he had imagined to find all the animals he wanted to speak to, to spread the word, but he was pleased. He was especially pleased that he had found Matahari. The conference would be tomorrow night, in the glade next to the waterfall. Sure that all those who mattered in the forest would be there, he squatted contentedly in the tree, shoulders hunched. At intervals, he would shake the rain off the thick long hair on his back. It rolled down, leaving him still dry. It was too risky to try and get back now. But he would head back to the kampong immediately as soon as it was dawn. He settled down for the night ahead.

When dawn finally tiptoed in, through the rising mist, Tunku was awake. Standing, he shook himself, and started to swing through the trees, a seemingly leisurely, effortless swing, his long arms reaching out and grasping easily lianas and vines by which he propelled himself onwards, forward. The rain had stopped, but the trees and foliage were still wet, glistening, dripping. It was cool. Every time he grasped a liana, a vine, he created a small shower of water. As the rising sun started to warm the cold, wet earth below, steam rose up and vaporised. High up in the forest canopy, Tunku was enjoying this. It was as if he was swinging through the trees above the clouds. It took him less than an hour to reach the kampong.

Puteri was greatly relieved to see him. They sat together on the platform, the baby between them. He told her that he had found Matahari, the Lord of all the elephants. Matahari had agreed to the conference which would be held tomorrow night. All the leaders of the forest animals would be there.

Then Ibrahim appeared, standing below, smiling up at them.

"Tunku." he called "You are back."

Tunku waved at him. Ibrahim climbed up on to his platform.

"You are well? I was worried."

In grunts and hoots, Tunku told Ibrahim that there was to be a Grand Conference in the forest the following evening.

"Oh good. I want to come too" said Ibrahim.

Tunku thought for a while before he nodded in agreement.

"But you must stay close to me, and only do as I say" he told Ibrahim. "There will be those there who will be suspicious of you. They are wary of humans."

"Can Joseph come, because he is sort of in charge?" asked Ibrahim.

Tunku frowned for a while. He sat silent, brooding. Then, eventually, he sighed and said

"Only if you take responsibility for him. He must do exactly as I say, and not speak a word."

"Tunku, thank-you. You won't regret this" cried Ibrahim happily, giving him a hug.

The children were all there, working with Yusof and Aishah, dressing wounds, feeding, cleaning the animals.

Yusof was pleased; the time had come for many of them to be released. They would have to be transported deep inside the forest, away from any potential harm from fires. He decided to ask the Orang Asli to help. No human knew the forest better than they did. The Orang Asli would find a safe haven for these poor creatures.

Gently he took the baby orang-utan from Puteri. First he examined its back and tummy. There were scabs there still, but they would drop off eventually, skin had already started to grow back, and soon the hair would grow too. The baby was very good, sitting quietly on Yusof's examination table. He unwound the bandages from its tiny hands, and then from its feet. All the horrible fried skin, cracked and charred, had healed. Yusof tested its fingers and toes; they all moved properly, they were still weak, but fine. He smiled at Puteri.

"Your baby's come through! He's going to be a fine young orang-utan."

Puteri looked him carefully in the eye. He knew what she was communicating.

"There, there" he said, awkwardly patting her hand.

After lunch, Yusof went off into the forest to find the Orang Asli.

With some of the money Mr Brown had raised, Aishah had bought more seeds and new young vegetable shoots. She went off with Faradilla and Xin Hui to plant them. They harnessed the buffalo, attaching the plough, and off it went, Aishah steering the plough, Xin Hui watering the ground behind her, and Faradilla, behind Xin Hui, casting seeds into the newly ploughed furrows. Then all they had to do was to turn the soil over the newly sewn seeds so that they were not devoured by birds. After that, they planted the vegetable shoots. This was harder work, bending down, planting each one individually. Faradilla had been helping her mother since she could walk, but, for Xin Hui, it was a novelty. She was tired, and her back felt as if it were breaking, but she was having such fun! *'Just wait 'till I tell Mummee what I've been doing!'*

CHAPTER 7

It was dusk. Ibrahim and Joseph were tense, nervous, and excited. They padded silently along the shadowy path towards the edge of the mangrove swamp where they were to meet Tunku. There was very little sound; the noise of crickets calling, the creaking of bending branches in the trees, an occasional snapped twig. The atmosphere in the forest was heavy with tension. Something was afoot.

"Watch out for crocodiles" hissed Ibrahim.

"And snakes hanging from the branches" he added, as an afterthought.

Warily, Joseph scoured the ground around him. Then he scanned the tree branches above his head. There was nothing there. He padded on, behind Ibrahim, not letting him out of his sight. There was a loud hoot directly overhead. Joseph's heart thumped frantically.

"It is Tunku" Ibrahim called keeping his voice low.

CHAPTER 7

Tunku swung down from the tree. He communicated with Ibrahim who, turning to Joseph, said

"We must hurry. We cannot be late. Tunku will carry us to save time."

"Carry us? How?" whispered Joseph.

"On his back. We have to cling on, one of us at each shoulder."

"Uhu, I can't do that" said Joseph, stepping back in horror.

"Stop! Don't move!" cried Ibrahim.

Joseph froze in his tracks.

"There's a snake hanging down behind you. It's a deadly one. Just walk forward, very very slowly" said Ibrahim softly.

Joseph walked slowly forward, ten paces.

"That's enough" said Ibrahim. "Danger over!"

Turning round, Joseph saw a large black snake with yellow diamonds disappearing up the trunk of a tree. Now that the danger was over, he started to tremble.

"We have no choice" Ibrahim said. "If we want to attend the conference, we must go with Tunku. It will be alright, you will see."

Grabbing Joseph's hand, he pulled him towards Tunku who was sitting patiently on the ground, waiting. He was wiggling his toes, watching them with fascination. Tunku's hands and feet were disproportionately large compared to his body size. Long, slim, and very strong, they were designed for climbing, clinging on to trees and branches. Ibrahim pulled a strong liana down. They climbed on to Tunku's back. His red, glossy coat was

thick and long. His shoulders were broad. There was plenty of room for Joseph to wrap his fingers firmly through the hair on top of Tunku's shoulders. Ibrahim tied the liana around them, passing the strands to Tunku, who tied them firmly across his own belly. Like Joseph, Ibrahim threaded his fingers through the hair on Tunku's shoulders.

"Comfortable?" asked Ibrahim. Joseph nodded, too scared to speak.

With that, Tunku started to climb a nearby tree. Quickly, he reached the top, the forest canopy. Grabbing a liana, he started to swing. Joseph's eyes, shut tight initially, opened wide. The forest below was gliding silently past. They were swinging right up in the top of the Dipterocarp, giants of the forest. It was clearer up here, lighter, not so much vegetation. Down below it was darker, dense, but he could still see creatures making their way along the forest paths and trails, cats, lizards, porcupines, crocodiles even, all heading in the same direction. He could see the undergrowth and the clearings, the rivers, the ponds and lakes. He was free as air. This was flying. It was great! He grinned at Ibrahim, who was grinning back. Tunku gathered speed. The boys clung on. Joseph, gaining courage, looked around. There were other creatures flying through the trees, more orang-utans, macaques, all manner of other monkeys, squirrels, birds. Tunku, even with the burden of two children on his back, was overtaking them all. Ibrahim rolled his eyes at Joseph, indicating that he should look down. Joseph did so. Down below there were tens of elephants, big ones, middle-sized ones, even babies, all heading towards the glade. Rolling gait, trunks swinging, rumbling quietly, they padded along, babies clinging with their trunks to their mothers' tails. He spotted a family of rare rhinoceros, even a tiger. Joseph was filled with wonder. Ibrahim laughed gleefully.

"This is my world. Don't you love it!" he shouted.

CHAPTER 7

The closer they got to the glade, the more animals they saw on the move, all heading in the same direction, like them, towards the glade. Tunku and Matahari between them had done a good job. Soon, they saw the waterfall ahead. It was a splendid sight, much higher than the trees, millions of gallons of water thundering over it, crashing into the pool below. It was powerful. As they approached the glade, Tunku slowed down and swung gently downwards through the several layers of forestation, until they were at the edge of the glade. He untied the supporting liana, and there they were, standing on the ground. Joseph's knees were wobbling. He rubbed his eyes. He could not believe what he saw in front of him. Hundreds of animals of every kind had converged on this place. But, right at the front of all of them was the most enormous elephant he had ever seen. Matahari was so grey he was almost black. He stood several feet higher than any other creature there. His tusks were so long they nearly touched the ground. They gleamed eerily in the moonlight. His great head and ears swung slowly from side to side as he surveyed the crowds of animals, taking everything in. Tunku, bending down, picked Joseph up and placed him on a tree branch above the heads of most of the animals. Bending again, he scooped Ibrahim up and placed him firmly alongside Joseph.

"He says we are to keep absolutely quiet, and not move a muscle" said Ibrahim.

Merging into the vast gathering of animals, Tunku quickly disappeared. Ibrahim and Joseph looked around in wonder. The glade was full from side to side. It was dark, but the glade was well lit. Hundreds of fireflies, who lived in the mangrove swamp on the other side of the river, had obligingly flown across and lit up the glade. Like tiny fairy lights, they flickered overhead.

Ibrahim nudged Joseph and pointed; in the far corner of the glade, they saw the head man of the Orang Asli and a couple of his elders. 'So, they are here too! This is big.' thought Joseph. There were so many elephants, bears, cats, rhinos,

and every other animal, large and small that Joseph could not even begin to count.

The head man moved towards Matahari. The boys could now see that Tunku was there as well. They were communicating, gesticulating, the head man occasionally banging the shaft of his spear on the ground. Tunku pointed towards the boys sitting in the tree. Joseph froze. Then the head man and elders nodded, and Matahari rumbled loudly, tossing his great head. Tunku started to make his way back towards the boys in the tree. When he got there, he lifted them down gently, and gestured for them to climb on his back.

"What is it, Tunku?" Ibrahim asked.

"He says we've got to tell them what's happening, because we know it best" said Ibrahim. "He's taking us to the other side of the glade. There's a hillock there we can stand on so they can all see us".

"Oh, no. I'm scared" cried Joseph.

"So am I. But they're all watching. What else can we do?" He shrugged.

They climbed on to Tunku's back once again and were carried swiftly to the hillock where Matahari and the head man were waiting for them. Up close, Matahari looked even bigger and more terrifying and the head man and elders looked no less fierce. Tunku placed the boys on the hillock.

"We have to tell them" said Ibrahim. "I shall start, but I want you to tell them about the evil palm oil baron, and what we're going to do, because you know more."

:

"Uhu!" Joseph was so nervous, he wondered whether he would be able to speak at all. It seemed as if all the residents of the forest were here, in this glade. The boys turned to face them. Matahari trumpeted a mighty blast. Joseph jumped.

Tunku and the head man nodded at them. Ibrahim cleared his throat.

"Creatures of the forest" he started "mighty and small, strong and weak, we need your help. The evil palm oil baron wants to burn the forest down, he wants to burn my kampong down. He intends to fire the forest in two weeks' time. You all know he has already taken a lot of our forest, our land, to plant palm oil. Many of us have lost friends and family to the fires."

He stopped to take a breath.

"I know many of you, because of the fires already started, are crippled, lame, in need of support from your families. We believe this man is greedy and evil. We intend to stop him. We want you to help us stop him. If you help us, we can do it. My friend, Joseph, will tell you about our plan."

The creatures shuffled their feet, swayed, murmured in unison.

Ibrahim gestured to Joseph. Clearing his throat several times, Joseph eventually began:

"Ibrahim is right. The evil palm oil baron wants more and more land to plant palm oil because he makes lots and lots of money from it. He does not care about the forest, the creatures, the plants; he does not care about the kampong and the villagers who live there.

We want to build a fire-break fifty feet into the forest where it won't be seen by the evil palm oil baron's workmen. If they see it, they will try to stop us. It must be five miles long and fifty feet wide, and we have only two weeks to do it. If we make it deep enough, when it rains, the rain water will stay there, in the fire break, which will make it even more effective. The villagers are going to help us. Yusof has organised that. But, even with their help, we cannot do it quickly enough. We need your help as well, to clear away the undergrowth, to dig, to clear away the scrub, and we have to do it all in secret. If this is going to work, we shall have to work together, day and night. Will you help us?"

Joseph had not taken a single breath throughout his speech. Completely winded now, he stopped speaking. He stood, head down, struggling to get his breath. Eventually, sheepishly, he raised his eyes and looked warily around.

The creatures were shuffling and weaving, softly communicating with each other. Lowing, hooting, mewing, clicking, barking, rumbling, grunting, there were so many noises. The head man climbed the hillock and stood beside Ibrahim and Joseph. He smiled at them. Joseph nearly fainted. The elders followed. Tunku came and stood beside them, and Matahari, swaying slightly, lifted his trunk in salute. He trumpeted.

"These children, even with the support of the villagers, cannot fight this evil on their own. I commit my tribe to their support. We shall work together to defend our forest."

There was a roar from all the creatures, calling in agreement. They were in harmony. They would support the children.

Joyfully, Ibrahim and Joseph, all fear now forgotten, hugged Tunku and, bowing low, thanked both him and Matahari for organising the conference. Matahari rumbled at Ibrahim.

"Tunku is tired now, so Matahari will carry us to the edge of the forest on his back" Ibrahim said.

"Wow! An elephant ride! Oh great! I can't believe this. Nobody will believe it." cried Joseph.

Matahari lowered his trunk inviting Ibrahim to climb on. Joseph watched whilst Matahari carefully lifted his trunk and deposited Ibrahim on his back. Then it was his turn. Joseph thought he might be in heaven. Tunku hooted, and disappeared up into the highest canopy. The other creatures had already started to disperse, swiftly, silently. Turning, Matahari padded along the forest trails, his soft footfall scarcely denting the forest floor.

Joseph had never ridden an elephant before. He was enjoying the gentle swaying motion. He felt safe and secure on Matahari's broad black back. They did not seem to be travelling fast, but Matahari was covering a lot of ground very quickly. In no time at all they emerged from the forest. They were on the edge of the kampong. The stars were shining brightly above them. There was a full moon.

"Look. There's a shooting star" cried Ibrahim, pointing. 'This is probably a dream.' thought Joseph. "I think it's just a beautiful magical dream." Matahari lifted them off his back with his trunk, one by one. Ibrahim stood by him for a few moments, whispering to him. Joseph wondered what he was saying. Then, turning, Matahari melted into the forest. The two boys were alone.

"Come" Ibrahim whispered. Quickly and quietly they made their way through the kampong, trying not to disturb the sleeping dogs. On reaching Yusof's house, Katak emerged to greet them, tail wagging, but he did not bark.

"It's as if all the dogs know not to bark at us" whispered Joseph.

"They do."

"How was it that, when I spoke, all the creatures understood?"

They settled down on the anjung, curling up on clean sheets of coconut matting, Katak firmly wedged between them.

"That's the magic of the forest" whispered Ibrahim before he fell into a deep sleep.

CHAPTER

The following morning, Yusof was up at dawn. Today would be a busy day. He smiled as he stepped over the comatose bodies of the two sleeping boys on the anjung. He had some idea of what they had been up to the previous night, but he had faith in Ibrahim. He knew that Ibrahim would always be well taken care of in the forest. And Joseph, too, as his friend. The creatures would see to that.

He made his way to the animal enclosures. Calling, he told the animals that many of them would go back to the forest today, that the Orang Asli were coming to show them the way deep into the forest, where they would be safe from fires. They would carry those who were too infirm or too slow to manage such a distance alone.

Those animals who were fit, restless now that they were recovered, stirred impatiently in their various pens, cages, holes. Those who had been shut in, for their own safety, were released. In no time at all the padang was seething with creatures, yawning, stretching, scratching, strolling, or just sitting. All of them were waiting for the Orang Asli. They were grateful to Yusof for having helped them, but now they wanted to be off, back to their own environment.

And then the Orang Asli were there, in their midst. They had constructed papoose-style open-weave baskets into which they placed the lizards, the loris', the snakes, and any others who would be slow on foot. They had small finely woven baskets for the insects, the caterpillars, bees, ants, beetles, millipedes and centipedes, butterflies, moths, and all the others. They slung the baskets on to poles, which they carried balanced on their shoulders.

The head man and the elders were talking quietly to Yusof in a corner of the padang. Yusof shook his head, as if in disbelief. He frowned. He appeared agitated. And then he started to smile, a big broad smile and, throwing back his head, he burst into laughter. He was laughing so much that his body rocked. The head man was telling him what had happened at the conference the previous evening. The Orang Asli, even as they worked amongst the animals, efficient and quiet, were all smiling too.

It was a strange procession which formed on the padang. The head man and elders were at the front, several of the Orang Asli were behind, poles laden with baskets swinging across their shoulders. Interspersed with the Orang Asli were cats, monkeys, apes, lizards, and many others. Faradilla's little civet cat was there. And then a few Orang Asli brought up the rear – to scoop up those for whom the journey would be too much.

Tunku and Puteri were there, Puteri holding her baby close, and Number One Son by her side. Puteri's baby's hands were still not as strong as they should be, so she had decided to walk with the Orang Asli rather than ask her baby to hang on if she flew through the canopy. She would find the walk long and hard, but, if necessary, Tunku would return and relieve her.

Tunku and Number One Son climbed up into the canopy accompanied by the monkeys, the gibbons, the macaques, flying squirrels, bats, birds of all kinds. One of the Toucans was being particularly raucous. Tunku told him to be quiet. They did not want to draw attention to themselves.

And then, just as they had come, the Orang Asli melted into the forest, along with all the creatures. Darkness had not yet lifted. The nightly mist had not yet risen from the ground. Yusof stood in the middle of the padang, alone. The creatures and Orang Asli might never have been there. Sighing, he headed for home, for breakfast. The animal enclosures could be cleaned out later.

Aishah had left the boys to sleep on the anjung, but she and Faradilla had already prepared breakfast. As they ate, Yusof told them that all the animals who were well enough, had gone. The Orang Asli had taken them. Faradilla was sad. She would miss her civet cat. Katak, understanding her sadness, snuggled up to her. He nuzzled her face with his wet nose. She gave him a hug. No civet cat would really take his place in her affection.

There were still many animals left. Yusof was concerned about the monitor lizard. It was in great pain. It had become arthritic, its temper had not improved, and he felt that it might never be able to return to the forest.

Aishah said

"If Mr Brown is right, and we can start a charity, perhaps we can keep these animals, those who are too sick to return, and look after them here. We might be able to afford it. We could establish a shelter. Every day, the villagers are still finding creatures which need our help."

"I should like to do that" said Yusof "but the fact remains that the evil palm oil baron is about to burn down our kampong. And what would we do with the animals then? That is my concern."

"The children will organise the digging of a fire-break..."

"Have you any idea what an enormous task that is? I admire their spirit, but I think it is a dream. The head man has told me that Ibrahim and Joseph went to a conference of the animals in the forest last night. Tunku and Matahari organised it. And they all want to help. But I don't know! We only have two weeks." he ended.

Aishah and Yusof, dejected, drank their tea in silence. Faradilla held on tight to Katak.

On the anjung, Ibrahim and Joseph stirred. Sitting up, they stretched and yawned before rising, showering, and then joining Aishah, Ibrahim and Faradilla for breakfast.

"And where were you last night?" Yusof asked.

"Ayah we have so much to tell you" answered Ibrahim. He was bubbling with excitement.

"You won't believe it" said Joseph. "I still think I've been dreaming. I can't believe it's happened."

"It happened." said Yusof. The Orang Asli came this morning and took the able animals to a safe place in the forest. The head man told me."

"The animals have gone?"

"Yes, they have gone, those that are fit enough. There are still many left."

"It seems you two boys made quite an impression last night. You are very lucky, very privileged, you know. It is rare for humans to witness such events. The elders of the

CHAPTER 8

Orang Asli are allowed to attend, because they, too, are forest dwellers. But generally, nobody else ever sees such a thing. I doubt you will see it again. You must not tell a soul about this, otherwise the forest will be full of curious people trying to see for themselves, and it will destroy the creatures. I want your solemn promise that you will tell nobody."

Yusof looked very serious.

"Faradilla knows. What about Vinod and Xin Hui?"

"Well, I suppose you will have to tell them but they must also be sworn to secrecy."

"Yes , Ayah. We will tell nobody."

"Yes, uncle Yusof, of course we won't. I swear!"

They ate their breakfast with gusto! They were very hungry. After breakfast, Xin Hui and Vinod arrived on their bikes.

"Hi, everyone" called Vinod, as he hurtled towards them, Xin Hui in close pursuit.

"We've got so much to tell you, but you've got to keep it secret" Joseph called.

The children gathered together in a huddle. Aishah and Yusof went off to attend to their chores. Vinod was upset that he had been left out the previous evening.

"But" said Joseph "there was room on Tunku's back for only two of us. We would have liked you to come, but there was no room."

Vinod had to agree that he was right. "My Mum's having a new baby soon." he said.

"Anyway" chipped in Ibrahim, " the animals and the Orang Asli are going to help us dig the fire-break. That is the important thing. And we are going to start tomorrow."

Vinod cheered up immediately.

"We must all tell our parents tonight" said Joseph, "and get them to help us as much as they can."

"My parents are city people, lah" said Xin Hui. "They will not know what to do."

"They'll be able to do something. Everybody can do something. Tomorrow is Saturday, so the parents won't be working. We must ask them to bring spades, shovels, axes, cutting tools, anything they can to help cut down the trees and the undergrowth."

"Come on" said Ibrahim. "We'll help my father clean out the animal quarters, and then we'll gather together all the tools we can find. We shall need everything."

Two hours later, the children, having thoroughly cleaned out the animal quarters, were searching for tools – everywhere they could think of.

"Ayah, how many villagers are coming to help us?" asked Ibrahim.

"We'll have to see" said Yusof, "but I think there will be about thirty or forty, and there will be just as many Orang Asli. Don't worry about tools for them. They will bring their own."

"We must go now" said Joseph. Turning to the others, he said "We've got to speak to the Imam first."

They set off on foot. It was not far to the mosque, and then the Buddhist temple and the Hindu temple were a stone's throw away, and the Church was just around the corner.

Arriving at the mosque, the five children took their shoes off and entered. It was a pale shade of blue all over, outside and inside, totally bare, just a few mats on the floor. *Strange*, thought Joseph, accustomed to all the trappings of the Catholic Church, There were a few people on their knees on the mats, all wearing their white caps, praying, but that was all. Ibrahim led them towards a small room at the back of the mosque, walking around the central part. There they found the Imam. He was a very wise man, Ibrahim had explained, but he looked quite scary with his wide black turban, thin face, and long white beard. He wore funny little rimmed spectacles and a long black robe. He sat cross-legged on the floor. Ibrahim knelt down in front of him. The others copied Ibrahim. Ibrahim explained to him what they were doing, how they needed more people to help them save the forest and the animals. He spoke for some time. The Imam listened gravely, patiently, in silence, without interrupting. Ibrahim finished. He sat, waiting, breathing hard. And still the Imam said nothing. The children held their breath. Finally the Imam spoke "You children mean well. I feel you are doing the right thing, and so I shall request that as many as possible will help you."

"Thank you, Imam" Ibrahim said "We gather at the kampong at dawn tomorrow". The Imam picked up his Qu'ran, and the children, rising, backed out of the room.

Quickly, they slipped their shoes on and headed towards the Buddhist Temple, which was just a couple of doors down the road where, once again, they removed their shoes before entering. This building was quite different from the mosque. Heavily ornate, painted dragons prancing on the roof, gold leaf gilded relief carvings everywhere, beautiful paintings on the walls, on the ceiling, a huge incense burner in the middle of the temple, a huge golden statue of Buddha, and the wonderful pungent smell of joss sticks. There were several altars to different gods, to Ma Zhu Po, the goddess of the sea, to Yue Gong Niang Niang, the moon goddess, Ri Gong Tai Zi, the sun god, and Guan Yin, the goddess of mercy. It was bewildering to Joseph, who had no knowledge of gods and goddesses. For him there was only one God. But this was Xin Hui's territory. Xin Hui lit a joss stick first, in front of the main alter, and holding it between her joined hands, she bowed several times, muttering, then, placing the joss stick in a holder alongside many others, she padded happily towards a saffron-robed, round-faced monk who was sitting at the side of the temple on a small stool, in front of a low table. He wore spectacles too, but his were round, just like his face. He smiled happily at the children.

"And what can I do for you, children?" he asked. He turned towards another monk and said something, whereupon the monk disappeared, and returned, bringing with him five cups of water, which he presented to the children. They drank thirstily. Joseph looked expectantly at Xin Hui and she, in her piping voice, began. She talked, hesitantly at first, but, becoming more confident by the minute, she gathered pace until, rounding off, she said "…. and so, you see, we need all your help, and the help of all the Buddhist people, to save the forest and the animals. Oh, and the plants too, lah, because they are so precious."

The monk chuckled. He patted her on the head.

"You are quite right. The preservation of life, of all life, is our most important task on this earth. I shall see to it that there are people to help you in the morning, at the Kampong." With that, he opened his arms wide, as if to envelope all the children, and herded them towards the exit. As he waved goodbye to them, he was still chuckling.

The children's next port of call was the Hindu Temple which like the Buddhist Temple, was very ornate, but in a different way. The external walls were topped with carvings of sacred cows. There were so many carvings of gods, all painted in vivid, bright colours, that it looked as if they were climbing on top of each other. Garlanded with fresh flowers, Kali, Shiva, Ganesh, who was half elephant, half man, and painted blue, and lots of other gods, some half animal, half human, some riding peacocks, and all manner of weird creatures – there were so many gods. And the temple was full of sound, drums, horns, and bells. Fragrant incense, blessed fire, and offerings of fruit, grain and sweets at each of the altars; holy men, dressed only in loin cloths, and with their heads and bodies covered in ash were accepting offerings from supplicants, sometimes handing out bananas in return. The temple was busy, and very bewildering for the children, but Vinod knew what he was doing. He led the way towards an emaciated looking holy man sitting at the shrine to Kali, the Goddess of fearlessness.

"This is a priest" he said. He spoke to the priest who, distracted, was not paying him any attention until Vinod tugged at his arm. The man turned towards him, holding out a banana, but Vinod shook his head.

"I want to talk to you" he said. "Please listen". At that, the holy man raised his shoulders, and turned towards a quiet corner of the temple, followed by the children. Gesturing, he asked Vinod to say his piece. Vinod spoke clearly and precisely for ten minutes. The holy man let him finish. Then, after a pause, he said "You have my word. I will help you". Clearly a man of few words, he left them, and headed back towards the shrine of Kali.

"Whew!" said Joseph when they got outside. "That was odd". Vinod looked pained, and Ibrahim said kindly, "It's a lot more interesting than the mosque."

"Now we have to go to the Gurdwara".

"What's that?"

"It's my temple, the Sikh temple. We must ask the Granthi for help."

In the Sikh temple, which was really quite bare, Vinod found the Granthi and again, clearly and precisely, explained what they were doing and their need for help.

"I will notify the committee" said the Granthi. "I think you will find that you have the support of the Sikh community.

The children chorused their thanks, and off they went.

"It's just the priest now" said Joseph. This was his territory. He was confident here. They entered the Church, Victorian gothic in style, painted white on the outside "Like a wedding cake" said Xin Hui. Inside, all was calm. A sense of peace was all-pervading. Pews lined up symmetrically on either side of a wide aisle, which had a big altar at the far end, surmounted by a huge golden crucifix. The ceiling was high, gothic. Joseph knew where to find the priest. He headed towards the presbytery behind the altar. At that moment, the priest came out.

"Why, hello Joseph" he said. "I see you have brought your friends with you." He smiled kindly at the children.

"Father, we need your help" said Joseph without preamble.

"You had better sit down" said the priest, indicating one of the pews. The children filed in. "Now, what can I do for you?"

Joseph launched into his story, telling it all, except the bit about the conference in the forest glade, and the involvement of the animals. No grown-ups (apart from Yusof) would ever believe him.

"Hmm!" said the priest when Joseph had finished "Well, I might be able to help you. It is a good thing that you are doing. You know that, don't you?" He looked at the children.

They were vulnerable, young, a couple of them very small, taking on the big palm oil baron. *'Plucky little kids!'*

"I shall be at the kampong tomorrow morning, and I have no doubt that I can bring several others along as well. Does that help?"

"Oh yes, Father" said Joseph gratefully.

The children left the Church feeling very pleased with themselves. The Imam, the Monks, the Hindu priest, the Granthi, and the Catholic priest had all agreed to help them. They strolled down the road.

"What's happening about the e.mails?" asked Vinod.

"I don't know. All the replies should be sent to the evil palm oil baron, but I don't know whether its working or not." replied Joseph.

"Lots of my friends have sent them" said Xin Hui.

"So have mine" chorused the others.

"We'll soon know whether it's having any effect" said Joseph grimly. "We can check tonight, but do not sit at your computers for too long. Do not forget that we all have to have an early night. Tomorrow's going to be a big day." Joseph felt very responsible.

CHAPTER 9

They were up at the crack of dawn. This was to be the first day of work on the fire-break. The parents had all agreed to come too, and they were bringing friends. Each family loaded as many tools as they felt would be useful into the boot of their car. Mr Chan had gone out and bought a shiny new shovel (small size) for Mrs Chan, and an axe for himself. He had bought some nice strong gardening gloves for Mrs Chan and Xin Hui, so that they would not hurt their hands. He had bought them all some sturdy walking boots, and they wore long trousers, to protect their legs. Mr and Mrs Singh brought tools and Mrs Singh, sensibly, brought a first aid kit, with lots of plasters and disinfectant. Mr and Mrs Brown brought spades, shovels, secateurs, shears, and several cases full of bottles of drinking water. It had already been agreed that they would not use electrical tools, which would be noisy, and possibly attract the attention of the evil palm oil baron's men.

Very early in the morning, they gathered on the padang in front of Yusof's kampong. The villagers were already there. Several of the women had started preparing lunch for everyone. Those women not involved in preparing lunch had tucked up their sarongs, ready for action. All the men carried spades, axes, saws. It was uplifting for the children to see so many grown-ups ready to help them. Gradually, more and more arrived. Ibrahim spotted members of his mosque. Yusof and Aishah greeted them. The Imam had kept his word. Xin Hui and Mr and Mrs Chan were delighted to see many Buddhist monks there, all in their saffron robes, tucked up, ready prepared with tools. Vinod and Mr and Mrs Singh felt vindicated when about thirty Sikhs arrived. Tall men, wearing turbans, with moustaches and beards; they looked fierce. Mr and Mrs Brown warmly greeted the Catholic priest and several members of his congregation. And then a whole trouple of Hindu men marched onto the padang. They were strong, wiry men.

The Orang Asli arrived, stealing silently out of the forest on to the padang. Mrs Chan gasped when she saw them. She reached out for Mr Chan. She had never, in all her life, seen such fierce looking people. They were terrifying. Mr Chan, himself, was a little worried. Mr Singh was very happy that, as a Sikh, he always carried a dagger about his person, just for self-defence! Quietly, he pushed Mrs Singh behind him.

"It's alright Mummee, Daddee" said Xin Hui. "They do a lot to help uncle Yusof and the animals, lah. And it's their forest, too, lah, so they're worried, more than we are."

Yusof, standing on the verandah of his house, started to speak.

"You have all kindly come here today to help the children build a fire-break, to prevent the evil palm oil baron from burning down any more forest and from burning down our kampong. I want you to understand that you are taking risks. If the evil palm oil baron finds out what we are doing, there could be a lot of trouble. Do not feel that anyone will think less of you if you leave us. It is too much to ask anyone to take such risks if they have any doubts."

The crowd on the padang (for it had become a crowd) shouted that they wanted to be there, to save the forest, to save the kampong. Joseph, Ibrahim, Vinod, Xin Hui, and Faradilla looked about them in wonder. There were Muslims, wearing their little caps, the women modestly covering their arms and legs, there were fierce warrior-like Sikhs with turbans and long beards, and Hindus looking just as fierce; there were Buddhist monks, country folk, city folk. As if the whole world was there!

"I would like Joseph to come up here and speak to you. After all, this is Joseph's idea."

Mrs Brown beamed with pride at her son as he made his way towards the anjung. Joseph called Ibrahim up beside him.

"Thank you all for coming" Joseph began. "As you know, we want to protect the forest. Uncle Yusof and villagers, our parents, and the Orang Asli, all of you, I thank you for coming here today. We have only two weeks to dig the fire-break. It will be hard work, but the creatures of the forest will help as well, so we do have a chance."

Mrs Chan looked at Mr Chan. "The creatures of the forest? What does he mean?" she whispered.

"I don't know." He shrugged.

Joseph had unfurled a home-made map on the anjung for everyone to see. His father, Mr Brown, had helped him make it at home the previous evening.

"You'll see from this map where we are going to dig the fire-break. It will be fifty feet in from the edge of the forest."

He did not know what else to say. Despairingly, he looked at Yusof. Yusof came up on to the anjung and stood beside Joseph.

CHAPTER 9

"I have already divided us into shifts. Some of us have to go to work during the day, but have volunteered to help in the early morning, or in the evening. We must work quietly so as not to attract the attention of the evil palm oil baron's men. You must not be afraid when you go into the forest and find the creatures there. They will be waiting for us. They are going to help us. The forest belongs to them, and they wish to protect it. So, let us begin."

He made his way down the anjung steps followed by Joseph. The villagers and volunteers fell in behind, the Orang Asli having already disappeared into the forest. They were a nervous, disparate group, carrying all manner of tools, but they followed Yusof along the small forest trail, until they reached the area where they would start digging the fire-break.

Matahari and his tribe were waiting for them, They rumbled a quiet greeting when they saw Yusof approach. Tunku, Puteri, Number One Son, and all their tribe were there, the gibbons and monkeys were there, up in the trees; on the ground there were pangolins, cats, civets, bears, even a few rhinocerous and wild boar, any creature which could knock down trees and brushwood, clear it away, or dig.

Aishah and the older women of the kampong had stayed behind to prepare lunch. But the younger women were there, alongside their menfolk.

The humans hesitated when they first saw the animals, but the villagers had lived with them for a long time, and soon relaxed. Those who lived in the city, Mr and Mrs Chan, Mr and Mrs Singh, and Mr and Mrs Brown amongst them, were rather more concerned. Mrs Chan was particularly frightened, but there was no way she could turn around and run back. Her legs would simply not have carried her; they were shaking so much. A young female elephant, sensing her distress, reached out and delicately, with the tip of her trunk, she nuzzled Mrs Chan's arm. Mrs Chan stopped breathing, she was rigid with fear, but then, when nothing terrible happened, she began to relax and when, eventually, she found the courage to look at the young elephant and saw her gentle eyes, Mrs Chan was able to smile. She reached out and stroked the elephant's trunk. The tip was pink, as were the tips of her ears, and she had white feathery hair growing out of her ears, and soft, tufty black hair on top of her head. *'She looks like a punk.'* thought Mrs Chan.

"Her name's Cahaya Bulan – it means 'Moonlight'" whispered Faradilla. Mrs Chan resolved that she would stay close to Moonlight.

The elephants took up their positions. There must have been fifty or sixty of them. They spread out, fifty yards apart, along the line of the fire-break. Each elephant was allotted a team of ten humans and ten other creatures. The elephants would uproot and knock down those trees along the line of the fire-break which it was absolutely necessary to knock down. They would pile the trunks up behind the line of the fire-break, creating a barrier of sorts, which would slow down the progress of the evil palm oil baron's men. The children, the apes and gibbons would drag away the underbrush, branches and leaves. The grown-up humans, pangolins, bears and cats, and boars would dig. Macaques, and birds in the treetops would keep a sharp look out for the evil palm oil baron's men. And so they began.

The largest elephants pushed, shoved and strained as they knocked down trees, the smaller elephants dragged them away and piled them up along the line of the barrier.

The humans dug with spades and shovels; pangolins, cats and bears dug with their claws, the wild boars rooted with their snouts; children, apes and monkeys darted back and forth removing undergrowth and piling it on top of the barriers. The rhinos pushed and shoved. Everybody was working hard. The only sounds were the rumblings of the elephant, metal scraping on stone, axes hacking at wood, the strained groans of falling trees, snapping of branches, grunting, heavy breathing, huffing, puffing. The dust raised was suffocating. Even in the forest

they could not escape the heat and humidity. People started to tie handkerchiefs around their mouths and noses. Mrs Singh busied herself distributing water bottles throughout the day. The Orang Asli, strong and hardened, were unaffected by the toil, but other humans were sweating profusely, sometimes gasping for breath. They worked on, bodies glistening, nobody slackened, until lunchtime.

Aishah had sent one of the young village girls to fetch them for lunch. Gratefully, the humans downed their tools and followed the girl back to the kampong. On the padang, Aishah and the village women had laid out a simple feast. There was Mee Siam (noodles with spicy sweet and sour sauce, eggs, grated peanuts and tofu), delectable salads, followed by fresh fruit – pineapple, mango, water melon, and lashings of delicious cold water. Everybody ate heartily. There was not much conversation. After they had eaten, then rested for twenty minutes, they set off again for the forest.

Refreshed by their lunch, the men attacked the undergrowth with renewed energy. Mrs Chan, having made her decision, stuck close to Moonlight, who was carrying away the fallen trees, to form a barrier. Mrs Chan carried brushwood, and did some digging too. She stopped, gratefully taking a bottle of water from Mrs Singh. Looking around, she could see Mr Chan, Xin Hui, and their friends, all busily working. It was very weird. She was no longer afraid. Humans and animals were working together, all in a common cause. It was something she never thought she would see. If anyone had told her this would happen, she would have laughed at them, thinking them mad. And now here she was. Wonders never cease! She picked up her shovel. She found herself working alongside a pangolin, digging with its claws. It was surprising to see how quickly it dug a hole.

Mr and Mrs Brown and their friends were in a team working with a big elephant called Ribut. Like Mrs Chan, once over the initial apprehension, they were perfectly relaxed at working alongside wild creatures of the forest. Grunting heavily as

she dug, stepping backwards, Mrs Brown bumped into one of the Orang Asli. She jumped out of her skin and squealed, but he merely grinned at her. Straightening her back briefly, she brushed her hair from her face, feeling a bit silly. She stepped sideways, and tripped over a tree root. She fell, heavily, on top of a boar which was digging enthusiastically. Like all boars, it was an irritable beast. It grunted angrily, shaking her off. She was convinced it was about to gore her. It seemed prepared to do so, but then it changed its mind, shook itself, and left her alone. She picked herself up hastily, vowing never to fall, stumble, or trip again. Mr Singh was there, too, working hard. He was swinging an axe rhythmically up and down, cutting tree trunks into smaller, more manageable pieces. Mr Chan and Mr Brown were busy hacking at the undergrowth, digging out the firebreak.

Yusof was working with Matahari. Matahari had lifted him on to his back, and, from that great height, he was able to see what was happening down the line, and give directions. The children were busy running backwards and forwards, dragging undergrowth out of the way. The three boys were useful. Their energy and enthusiasm made up for the lack of physical strength their fathers had.

And so villagers, city folk, wild men, and wild animals toiled alongside each other, working in perfect harmony, all day long, until dusk. The animals and Orang Asli departed, quietly melting once again into the forest. The humans made their way back to the kampong, tired, dirty, and aching, longing for a shower. Some had arrived in cars, some on motorbikes, some on bicycles, and many had walked. They set off for home. Every one of them had been touched, moved, by the events of that day, and was determined to return the following day.

The following day, they returned to the kampong, and the day after that, and the day after that. The toil was relentless, but, slowly, they were clearing the fire break. They worked on, until the fifth day. They had cleared, by now, over two and a half miles of the fire break. Everybody was working a little more slowly. The enthusiasm was still there, but they ached, their muscles, unaccustomed to all this hard exercise, were tired. They were becoming familiar with the animals, recognising individuals, occasionally brave enough to pat or stroke one. The animals and the Orang Asli, stoic as ever, toiled on.

Suddenly, Tunku cocked his head. In the far distance he could hear the loud boom and shriek of a Siamang calling. The Siamang were excellent forest rangers, travelling quickly through the trees, naturally inquisitive, all-seeing, all-knowing. The sound was picked up – another Siamang, nearer this time, and then another, even closer. The Orang Asli, whose hearing was also acute, heard it. It was the signal. Frantically, Tunku shook the branches around him, calling at the same time to Matahari and to Ibrahim. Matahari rumbled loudly. He was heard all the way down the line. It was the pre-arranged signal. Everyone, man and beast, stopped labouring, stood upright, looking about warily.

Apart from the natural forest sounds, the cicadas, there was absolute silence. They stood with bated breath, and waited. Nobody moved, neither man nor beast. Mrs Brown could hear the quiet, regular breathing of the bear she was standing next to. Then, borne on the wind, she thought she heard human voices. She turned her head towards the source. She saw nothing. The forest was dense. She strained to hear. But Matahari and Tunku had picked up the sounds, as had all the other animals. They turned their heads as one towards the area the sounds were coming from. It was the old dirt track, where the children had originally seen the evil palm oil baron's men. The Orang Asli were natural, trained stalkers. Taking Ibrahim with them, two of them set off silently, stealthily, towards the sounds, definitely recognisable now as voices.

The Orang Asli and Ibrahim reached the edge of the track. The two men pulled Ibrahim high up into the branches of a heavily canopied tree. Looking down, Ibrahim could see the length of the dirt track. Sure enough, some men were walking along it. He recognised a couple of them. One was the man he thought was the leader the last time he had seen them. Ibrahim did not know it, but this man was the evil palm oil baron's overseer.

"If that is what he wants, that is what we have to do." he was saying.

"But, Ah Kong, you know we cannot. We have not got the equipment. We cannot get it for another ten days. It's still at Kulamintang. You know that."

"We have to abandon Kulamintang then, for the time being. I dare not disobey the palm oil baron."

"And you say he wants us to clear *five hunded thousand* hectares, not two hundred? That is impossible. We cannot do it all at once."

Ibrahim started; he almost fell out of the tree. *'Five hundred thousand hectares*! Oh no! I must tell the others.'

"Yes we can. I have got some ideas" the overseer was grim. "I shall tell you later. But first we have to get those diggers, those caterpillars down from Kulamintang. How long will it take if you contact them today?"

"Well, they travel slowly. But they could be here in five days."

"Five days it is, then. We start in five days." They wandered on, slowly, down the dirt track.

Ibrahim and the two Orang Asli stayed where they were, in the tree, for another five minutes, making sure all was safe, before they finally climbed down.

"Quickly" he whispered to the two men. "We have to get back. I have to tell the others."

"Joseph, Vinod, Ayah, Matahari, Tunku" he called urgently as soon as they returned.

"It is bad news. That was the evil palm oil baron's men. Do not worry. They did not see us, and have no idea we are here, but they are going to start firing the forest in **FIVE** days', AND they are going to fire five hundred thousand hectares instead of two hundred."

Ibrahim was out of breath. The two Orang Asli had gone straight to the head man and the elders, and were clearly reporting the same news to them. Everyone stood silent, stunned. Their task appeared impossible. The fire break would have to be even longer, and they only had five days left. Ibrahim turned to Tunku and Matahari, explaining to them what he had already told the others. Joseph, who had climbed up on to Matahari's back, cleared his throat. In as loud a voice as he could, he said

"We must do our best. I think we should carry on."

Nobody questioned him. Taking up their tools, every man and woman bent their backs to the toil, and the animals, too, set to work. Nobody slackened.

Matahari trumpeted, and those further down the line took up the sound. The overseer and his men, walking further down the road, heard the elephants trumpeting in the forest. They had not realised the elephants were so close; it did not bother them. They laughed, believing the elephants would soon be gone, once the fires were lit. They envisaged the panicked, stampeding herd, and laughed all the more. Then they heard a tiger snarl. It was close by. Unsettled, the men picked up their pace. They had not been aware a tiger was in the vicinity. They headed quickly back towards their lorry.

Building the firebreak

CHAPTER 10

It was late in the evening. The children were sitting on the anjung again. It had become almost a way of life to them to spend the evenings here.

"What shall we do?" asked Vinod.

They were all silent, tired, depressed. The enormity of the task they had undertaken had dawned on them. So far, they had managed to keep going on pure adrenalin.

"We have got to send more e.mails out" said Ibrahim. "Tell more people what we're doing. They will support us, I know they will. Just think about the support we are getting right now."

"Yes. But if we do that, somebody will tell the newspapers, and then we shall have reporters swarming all over the place, getting in the way, tramping about in the forest." said Joseph. "I don't think the Orang Asli or the animals will like that."

"Will we be on T.V.?" asked Xin Hui excitedly. Faradilla's eyes widened in astonishment.

"I think we can send e.mails saying that the evil palm oil baron is about to burn down five hundred thousand hectares of forest, and we are fighting him with all our might to stop him, but we do not have to say how we are fighting him. We can say we need everyone's support."

"Can we ask the grown-ups to e.mail all their friends? I wish we were back at school. I am sure our schools would help, lah. How much more of the fire break have we got to dig? We have done a lot already," said Xin Hui.

"That depends on how they are going to approach things. If they spread out, right across the boundary of the forest, the fire break won't be long enough. But, if they concentrate on just this area, and try to burn from here, we should be able to hold them off."

"For how long? Will they not just try again, from somewhere else?" asked Ibrahim.

Joseph shook his head; he shrugged.

"We're only children. We can only do our best." He was tired. The sheer scale and audacity of what they were trying to do sometimes overwhelmed him.

"But the grown-ups are helping us. The Orang-Asli and the animals are helping us," said Vinod.

Joseph pulled himself together. "Come on. Let's go home. We'll send out e.mails to everyone, telling them what we are doing, but not where. We have to protect the forest. Is that OK?"

The children all nodded assent.

At home, the parents were too tired themselves to notice the children, sitting up late at the computers, sending out as many e.mails as they could.

Shirley Pooper was a reporter with the South East Asia Gazette. She was thinking. There were rumours afoot. Something was going on at one of the kampongs on the edge of the forest. She finished off her glass of wine. Perhaps she had better go and have a look. She would go the following morning.

It was about ten o'clock in the morning when Shirley arrived at the kampong. She wore high heeled shoes, a straight skirt slit up the back, and a fitted white blouse. Tall and thin, with pale blue eyes, her shoulder-length blonde hair was frizzy (the result of living in humid conditions), her cheap gold earrings jangled, her long finger nails were painted deep vermillion. She spotted the cars and bikes, parked neatly on the edge of the village. *'There must be at least a hundred cars here, and masses of bikes. Something's going on!'*

There were so many cars that she found it difficult to find a parking space. She tripped down the main street of the kampong, looking decidedly out of place. Several women were about, busily preparing lunch. But, otherwise, there was no sign that anything was afoot. She stopped one of the women, who was hurrying by carrying a big basket of freshly picked beans.

"What's going on here?" she asked. The woman smiled sweetly, gesticulated, and passed on. Shirley stopped another woman "Where are the people who own the cars?" Another smile, another gesture, and the woman passed on. Shirley was frustrated. *'Don't any of these people speak English?'* She wandered down the full length of the kampong street. The village dogs padded along behind her. At the end she found a house much larger, more imposing than the others. Beyond it were vegetable and fruit gardens, beyond those there appeared to be livestock, and beyond that was the forest. *'This must be the headman's house.'* She started to mount the steps. Katak came bounding towards her, hackles raised, barking. She stopped in her tracks. A slightly built woman emerged from the house. *'Gosh, what a beauty!'* The woman spoke softly to Katak who immediately stopped barking.

"Can I help you?" Aishah asked, in perfect English. She and Yusof had both studied biology at Oxford University which is where they had originally met and become friends with Professor Profundo.

"Yeah, I want to know what's going on here".

Aishah smiled. "As you see, there is nothing going on." She looked around her, at the other women bustling about. "We are engaged in preparing a mid-day meal. Can I offer you a drink, some lime juice perhaps?"

"Oh, yeah, thanks."

Aishah called into the house, and a younger woman emerged carrying a tray with a glass of cool, fresh lime juice. Shirley drank thirstily.

"Look" she said "It's nice of you to offer me a drink, but I need to know what's going on here. Something's going on. I've seen the cars. Where are the owners?"

"My dear, you really have no need to be concerned. As you see, there is nothing happening here." Aishah laughed. "I am sorry to have to disappoint you."

She was getting nowhere. Shirley took her leave, and headed off, up the kampong street, back to where the cars were parked. She thought she would take a look at the cars. She wandered among them, peering in through the windows. Would she find anything here? Some of the cars clearly belonged to wealthy individuals, but others were very ordinary. She was startled by a small boy who came running, threading his way through the cars. He was shrieking with laughter. Chasing him was a young orang-utan, who was actually grinning as he bounded along, knuckling the ground with his fists as he went. Then the boy turned. He started to chase the orang-utan. Shirley could swear she heard the orang-utan chuckle.

'Well, this is it! This is what they're up to. They're trading illegally in wild animals, selling them as pets.' Shirley was on to something. She determined to return, with a photographer this time. *'There's definitely something strange about this place.'* For the first time, she looked up at the treetops. She could see a lot of creatures up there – unusual so close to a kampong! A large fruit bat flew down, brushing the top of her head with its wings. Shirley squawked, ducking for cover. Running awkwardly towards her car, she wrenched the door open and climbed in. She was shaking. This could be, just could be, a big scoop. She really needed a scoop. Ever since Charlie Parsons had brought in the story of the aeroplane bomb intrigue, her boss reminded her every day that her job was on the line, unless she could come up with something. Besides, she was ambitious. She wanted to move on from the grotty little South East Asia Gazette. She wanted to work on the The Asian Times. To qualify for that, she needed to prove she could get a scoop.

She vowed to return to the kampong the following day with a photographer. She would not announce her presence, but would snoop around a bit. She drove off.

An hour later, the women of the village had laid out lunch in the padang, and the weary labourers made their way back from the forest to eat.

⁂

In England, Professor Profundo, an eminent botanist, was talking to his son, Toby. It was Sunday. They always had a lazy breakfast time together on Sundays.

"When did you get the e.mail? Yesterday? Well, perhaps we could look in to it. That's the third one so far?" He read the e.mail out loud.

"In our last two e.mails, we explained how the evil palm oil baron intends to burn the forest, and the kampong. He said he would burn two hundred hectares, but now it is five hundred thousand hectares. The creatures, the trees and plants in the forest are valuable. We are trying to save them. We are digging a fire break. Please e.mail the evil palm oil baron, ask him not to do this evil thing. Please forward this e.mail to all your friends."

"Umm, those children seem to be pretty determined. Burning the forest? We can't have that, can we!" He scratched the top of his bald head, watching Toby thoughtfully through spectacles perched on the end of his nose.

"Shall we take a trip to Malagiar, Toby? Have a look? I have always wanted to see a Rafflesia flowering in its natural environment. And I think I would like to have a look at some pitcher plants." He smiled.

Toby jumped up, gave him a hug. "Dad, you're the greatest."

"Let's see if we can book some flights. Find your passport, and pack a rucksack. Ah, I'd better tell your mother."

With that, the Professor trundled off to the kitchen. Mrs Profundo was accustomed to her husband's eccentric ways. Nothing would keep him away from his plants. She was quite happy for Toby to go too. It would be educational.

CHAPTER 11

Yusof was talking to the elders of the Orang Asli. The fire break, just about completed, was now five miles long. Joseph, Ibrahim, Vinod and Xin Hui were ecstatic. Faradilla would be pleased too, but she had stayed at home with Aishah today to help her mother prepare a special feast for everyone in the evening. The grown-up helpers and the animals were clearing away the last of the undergrowth. Yusof gestured the children to join him, and Tunku, and Matahari.

"No more can be done" he said "except pray for rain. What you children have achieved, what we have all achieved is amazing, but it may still not be enough. Ibrahim, tell Tunku and Matahari, they must ensure that all the young creatures, the sick and the old are taken deep into the forest where, if fires are started, they will not be affected."

Matahari turned towards the workers, who were resting. He trumpeted a great call. It signalled the end of all their efforts. The animals, rousing themselves, started, slowly, to depart. The humans were sad to see them go. Never, in all their lives, would they have believed (except the Orang Asli) that they would work alongside wild animals, in harmony, for the greater good. Mrs Chan gave Moonlight's trunk a big hug. "I do so hope we meet again" she whispered. Mr Chan put his arm around her shoulders. They watched as Moonlight turned and lumbered off silently, following her tribe. Ribut went with her. Mrs Brown wiped a tear from her eye. Joseph and Ibrahim clung to Tunku. He gently shook them off. And then he was gone, swinging through the trees.

All the humans stood respectfully to attention as the animals passed. They had worked so hard. And then the humans turned, shouldered their tools, and headed back, strangely silent, to the kampong, where Aishah and the other village women were waiting for them with a big feast laid out on the padang. They had put out flowers and little lanterns. Incense sticks were burning to keep the mosquitoes away.

Yusof, before he could join them, went off to tend those sick and burned animals still remaining in the kampong. Going through the vegetable gardens and the fruit gardens, he made his way towards the livestock area, and checked the cages, the pens. He fed the animals, watered them, checked their dressings, handling them gently.

Shirley Pooper, dressed more appropriately than the previous day, in slacks and sneakers, was hidden in the trees with her photographer. She tensed as Yusof approached, craning her neck to see what he was doing.

"Take that! Take that!" she hissed at the photographer, as Yusof carefully picked up the Monitor lizard and checked its burns. Gently, he applied more Aloe Vera before placing it back in its den. He moved on to a gibbon, which was also badly burned. Again, he handled it gently, applying the soothing Aloe.

"Have you got it?" hissed Shirley. The photographer, who was being eaten alive by mosquitoes and goodness knows what else, nodded assent. He was very uncomfortable. He

wanted to be back in town, swigging a long, cool beer in a bar.

Yusof moved on, deliberately tending the animals, feeding and watering them. Finally, he finished and headed back to the kampong to rejoin the others.

Shirley Pooper and her photographer, under cover of the trees, followed him. She rubbed her eyes when she spotted the padang. There must have been a hundred people there. What was it, a wedding feast? She could not tell. There were Muslims, Hindus, Buddhists, Sikhs, a Christian priest, and many villagers and townsfolk. Then she spotted the Orang Asli. She gasped. 'Savages! Wild savages!'

"Get that! Get that!" she hissed. She did not have to bother. The photographer was clicking away with his camera.

After washing, everyone settled down happily to eat and talk. They were exhausted, but pleased with what they had done. They ate, drank, and chatted well into the evening, unaware of the presence of Shirley and her photographer. They had dug a huge firebreak in record time and it was particularly special because they had been working alongside the creatures of the forest.

Up in the trees surrounding the padang were monkeys, gibbons and several others, always curious, watching the celebration below. It was one of the gibbons – a Siamang again –suspicious of Shirley and the photographer skulking in the undergrowth below – which boomed the alert. In no time at all the monkeys and apes set up such a ruckus. They hurled small objects- fruits, nuts and twigs at the pair. On the padang, the children jumped to their feet. They ran towards the edge of the gardens where Shirley and the photographer were scrabbling to get out of the undergrowth.

"Run! Run for the car!" Shirley screamed, as she tried to disentangle herself from a spiny thornbush. The photographer's camera strap had caught on the branches of another bush. He was trying desperately to disentangle it. The thorns scratched Shirley badly. She was bleeding profusely, and it hurt! "Ow, ow,ow!"she yowled. The photographer swore as, tugging hard, he broke the strap of his camera. *'I should not have agreed to this. That stupid woman! She is mad!'* He huffed and puffed. He tore his trousers, but did not notice. His hair was full of twigs and leaves.

Shirley Pooper and Bert were dragged by Joseph and Ibrahim, breathless, from the bushes, a sorry, dishevelled pair, torn clothes, scratched and bleeding, mud stained, covered in bits of undergrowth.

"Who are you?" demanded Joseph "What are you doing here?"

"N... nothing, just going for a walk" spluttered Shirley.

"At night? In the jungle?"

"Night photography!" chipped in the photographer.

"That's a fine story, but we do not believe one word of it." said Vinod.

Pulling herself to her full height, with as much dignity as she could muster, Shirley responded

"Who are you to question us? You're mere children. I know what you and your parents are up to. You're smuggling wild animals to sell as pets. I've seen them in the cages and pens down there. We've got it all on film." She was more confident now, smug even.

Ibrahim whispered to one of the gibbons.

"Is that true?" he asked. "Just what have you got on film?"

He had the attention of both Shirley and the photographer. Taking his cue, the gibbon moved in, unnoticed, and snatched the camera from the hands of the photographer. He galloped back to Ibrahim, swirling the camera around his head as he went.

"Hey! Give that back. That's private property" shouted the photographer, lunging at Ibrahim.

"I think you will find it is not." a strong, quiet voice out of the dark. Yusof emerged, followed by several others. "Please explain yourselves."

Surrounded now by several people, Shirley and the photographer were dumbstruck. Aishah moved forward. Taking Shirley gently by the arm, she led her to the house. Ibrahim and Joseph escorted the photographer. With a bowl of water and a soothing balm, Aishah gently washed and dressed their wounds, just as Yusof always did with the hurt animals. A monkey helped them pick the bits out of their hair.

"What are we to do with these people?" Ibrahim asked his father. Yusof smiled at his son.

"Why, as courtesy demands, we shall ask them to join us" he replied.

Joseph and Vinod exchanged astonished glances. Seeing them, Ibrahim smiled. "My father is right." Xin Hui and Faradilla, sitting on the verandah steps, took everything in.

"We shall take them" they cried and, jumping up, they held out their hands to Shirley and the photographer, whose name, he told them, was Bert. Xin Hui took Shirley's hand and led her down the steps, towards the padang. Faradilla took Bert's hand. *'What a tiny little thing'*. he thought. *'She's so pretty. Wish I had my camera! I must take a photograph of her – sometime!'* He remembered he no longer had his camera.

"Now you eat, lah" said Xin Hui, smiling at Shirley. She had led her to tables still laden with delicious, wonderfully fragrant food. Colourful dishes were laid out, inter-twined with vines and frangipani flowers. Little lanterns lit the tables. Lanterns were hanging in the trees. There was mee soup, roti, murtabak, nasi goreng, mee goreng, fried rice, satay, chicken briyani, prawns, chicken, and duck. There was lime juice to drink, lemon juice, watermelon juice and cold lemon tea. There were bowls of fresh fruit. *'What a feast. This has got to be something special. I'll get to the bottom of it yet.'* Shirley was still after her scoop. Bert was hungry. He tucked in with relish, remembering that he had not eaten all day. They sat down on rattan mats to eat (all the chairs had been taken), surrounded by the children.

Changing tack, conscious of her 'scoop', trying to be friendly, Shirley smiled at Xin Hui.

"This is a delicious feast" (said between mouthfuls) "What is it all for? Is it a wedding, or did you make a big sale of animals?" She still thought they were selling wild animals for profit.

Xin Hui looked at her long and hard. She did not like this silly woman with her painted nails and frizzy yellow hair.

'Perhaps she does not understand English'. **"What .is .this. feast for?"** Shirley asked, very slowly and loudly, gesturing towards the laden tables and the diners.

"It is the end of the day. We eat at the end of the day, lah." said Xin Hui.

"But this is not normal; this is special – all these people!"

"Yes" said Xin Hui.

Frustrated, Shirley turned towards Faradilla,

"Can you speak English?" Faradilla looked at her, big brown eyes unblinking under long lashes. Bert touched Faradilla's arm gently.

"Of course you speak English" he said, smiling. "I know you do." Faradilla smiled at him, a conspiratorial smile, but still said nothing.

Shirley Pooper was frustrated, tired and irritable. She had spent the whole day in seriously uncomfortable circumstances, getting bitten, scratched and torn, grappling with bushes, trees, tangled undergrowth, not to mention the insects, the bugs, the spiders, millipedes, centipedes, and goodness knows what else. She needed this scoop! She turned her attention to Joseph. At least he was European. He would definitely understand English.

"Who is that boy, the blond one?"

"It is Joseph" answered Xin Hui.

"Hey, you, Joseph, I want to talk to you" called Shirley.

Joseph turned towards her. Rising, he spoke to Ibrahim and Vinod, who both then rose with him. The three of them came over to Shirley, Bert, and the girls.

In her desperation for a 'scoop' Shirley blurted out her suspicions, thinking the children would unwittingly verify them. Bert simply carried on eating. He was tired of Shirley's nonsense, for he was sure it was nonsense. These were not evil, money-grabbing people.

Astonished, the children listened in silence, letting her finish. As usual, Joseph thought before he spoke. He sighed.

"So, what about the animals in the pens, down there?" she asked, pointing. "Are you planning to sell them?"

"What!?" the children chorused, not believing what they had heard.

"When will you sell the animals?" she persisted.

"You really do not understand, do you." said Joseph. "We are looking after them, healing them. They were all burned in the last fire. Yusof, Ibrahim's Dad, is healing them with herbs and balms he makes from plants in the forest. As soon as they are well enough, he releases them - back into the forest, of course. Can you imagine what it is like for the animals, to be suffocated by smoke, to be roasted slowly to death because they cannot move fast enough?"

Shirley shuddered, she was beginning to understand. Miraculously, she had pulled a notebook and pen from her pocket. This was too good a story to get anything wrong.

"Perhaps we should level with Miss Pooper. It would stop her getting other silly ideas. Well, we could tell her the basics." he said to the others. "She might be able to help us."

Shirley held her breath.

"Alright" said Ibrahim "We can tell her about the **people**." He emphasized the word 'people' to confirm their agreement that none of them would tell anybody about the involvement of the animals. The children nodded their agreement. So Joseph, Ibrahim and Vinod, with the girls chipping in, told her the story of the evil palm oil baron, his plans to burn down the forest and the kampong to plant more palm oil trees. Shirley scribbled as he talked. They told her how they had incorporated the help of the grown-ups, and, together, they were all trying to stop the evil palm oil baron. *'Oh ,my goodness, what a scoop. Shirley Pooper, this is your lucky day! Five hundred thousand hectares! This is big!'* Tiredness forgotten, she scribbled on, questioning, getting answers. They did not tell her how they had all dug a fire-break through the forest, to stop the fire. They did not tell her about the involvement of the animals.

"Those photos Bert took, they were mostly of that man - must be Yusof – handling the animals, yes, dressing their wounds. Can we have them back?"

"What else have you got on that film?"

"Not much, a few photos of the party here on the padang. But I want a photo of you children. After all, you seem to be the heroes in all this." said Bert.

The children liked his broad shoulders and gentle manner.

"What do you think, Faradilla?" asked Ibrahim.

"It's O.K." said Faradilla.

The children grouped together, and said "Cheese" into the camera lens. Little did they know that Bert was taking photos of them individually, as well as group photos. Eventually, he was satisfied.

They sat there, the children talking, Shirley scribbling, and Bert just listening, late into the night, when the grown-ups came and rounded them up for bed.

CHAPTER 12

Shirley Pooper was very excited, elated even. She had been busily typing up her notes. This was the beginning of a fair old story. She had checked the other newspapers that day; none had even a hint of the story. She wanted to keep it that way. By far the best part was that she had managed to negotiate an interview with the evil palm oil baron. In fact, she was about to see him this very afternoon. She had heard a lot about this man. He was very rich, very powerful, highly thought of by the government. She had got the interview by flattering him, telling him he was so great and powerful, she wanted his story. She would take Bert with her. She needed a photograph.

As they approached the fantastic building that was Universal Palm Oil Inc., Bert took photographs of it, artistic photographs, angling the shot through the fountains. The building was amazing; it was intimidating. It was meant to be. Shirley and Bert felt very small as they entered the huge marble and glass foyer, and as they went up in the glass lift to the penthouse suite.

This was the biggest interview Shirley Pooper had ever done. She quickly brushed the front of each shoe down the back of her leg, she tried to smooth down her skirt, and her frizzy hair. She licked her lips, and cleared her throat nervously.

The evil palm oil baron was waiting for them at the top of the lift. Having just had lunch with the Prime Minister, he was in a magnanimous mood; he reached out to Shirley, shaking her heartily by the hand, and then Bert. His hands were flaccid and fat, she noticed. Bert thought it would be good to take photographs before the interview, while the light was still good. So he did. He took photographs of the evil palm oil baron sitting at his big rosewood desk; he took photos of him standing against the glass windows with long views behind him of the palm oil plantation. He assured the evil palm oil baron that he would be able to airbrush out the large pink sticking plaster still on his head.

They chatted. The evil palm oil baron offered them a drink from his cocktail cabinet. Shirley refused. She never drank whilst working, she told him, but he was welcome to have a drink himself. He poured himself a large Malt whisky, lit a cigar, and settled down behind his desk.

"I believe you are the richest man in South East Asia?"

"Oh yes, I most certainly am. I own everything you can see for miles. I am so rich, I even own people." he laughed heartily. Shirley simpered.

"When do you think you will be able to say you have enough?"

He laughed again. This woman was priceless.

"Very funny! Very, very funny. You can never have enough. Look around you. All this costs money to maintain. I have a yacht and a private jet to maintain. I have four homes in four different countries, I have racehorses, I have a fleet of cars. I have a casino and a hotel to maintain. I have a very expensive wife and very expensive children. I have to entertain – government officials, you know. All very expensive!"

"A lot of people depend on me" he said archly. "They do not earn enough. Without me, they would be poor. Oh no, I can never have enough. In fact, this is just between us, you understand, I am about to plant another five hundred thousand hectares with palm oil"

The lunch with the Prime Minister had gone very well. He had agreed with the evil palm oil baron that it would be necessary to burn down another five hundred thousand hectares of forest. Of course, the evil palm oil baron had offered to lend the Prime Minister his yacht for a three week holiday, and the Prime Minister well knew that when he arrived on board the yacht, there would be an envelope waiting for him full of crisp clean dollar notes.

"What sort of people?"

"Oh, just people. I help a lot of people, you know. I am renowned for my benevolence."

"Do you mean that you bribe people, you bribe officials?"

Shirley did not know how she had found the courage to ask. Bert looked up, shocked. They watched, and waited, as the evil palm oil baron's smile disappeared. He went puce, and then a strange shade of purple. He pulled at the tie around his neck. The collar button was not done up. Reaching for his glass, he took a large swig of whisky.

" How dare you! How dare you come into my office and make allegations against me. You, a cheap newspaper hack like you!"

"S...sorry, sir" stuttered Shirley "I did not mean...." She did not get a chance to finish.

"Get out! Get out of my office," he roared.

Shirley and Bert scuttled out.

Standing outside the building, Shirley moaned that she had mishandled the interview. What a lost opportunity!

"Oh no" said Bert "Not if you got all that down, and, anyway, I heard it. I can remember most of it, you've got a real scoop. Did you not hear him? He virtually admitted he bribes people. He actually said he even owns people. O.K. he said it as a joke, but it is probably true. And he said he is about to plant five hundred thousand hectares of palm oil What he did not say was that he has first to burn down the forest. Those children were right."

"We had better get back to the office," Shirley was nervous "before he sends his henchmen after us. I am not going to tell the boss about this. He will freak." Shirley was shaking.

"I shall drive" said Bert. He started the engine, but the car stalled. He tried three times before he got it going. Looking back, over her shoulder, Shirley saw four very large, beefy men coming out of the building.

"Oh no. Hurry! Hurry!" she gasped.

Just in time, Bert got the car going.

On the way back, Shirley suddenly blurted out "That's it! The children were right. They said he was about to burn five hundred thousand hectares of forest, and he said he has government approval to plant five hundred thousand hectares of palm oil. It's the same five hundred thousand hectares. He virtually admitted he bribes people. What a horrible man!"

'Shirley Pooper, you are such a bright button.' thought Bert.

At the airport, Professor Profundo and Toby had touched down. They retrieved a couple of computers and several cameras from the overhead stow cupboards, and prepared to disembark.

"Where will we be staying, Dad?"

"What's that, Toby? Ah yes, we shall worry about that later. First things first. I think I shall pay a visit to my old friend, Yusof. I don't believe I have seen him for twelve years. We have kept in touch over the years, of course. He is doing some very interesting work, researching medicinal properties of forest plants."

Professor Profundo was looking forward to seeing his old friend again. Years ago they had done a lot of research together, very interesting research it was. Now, what was it they were researching? He could not remember, but, nonetheless, he had a lot of time for Yusof.

Going through Customs, they were stopped. Why did they carry so many cameras? Was this contraband? What was on the film? Professor Profundo dug deep into his pockets and eventually pulled out his passport, and various other papers confirming his identity as an eminent English Professor of Botany. He managed to assure the customs officials that the cameras were essential to his work. Toby breathed a deep sigh of relief as they finally passed through Customs. They hailed a taxi, and the Professor asked for Yusof's kampong. The taxi driver knew it.

"You visit Yusof, Sir? he asked.

Professor Profundo was surprised.

"Well, yes, indeed, I am visiting Yusof. He is an old and dear friend".

"He very good man. He do good work with medicines."

Clearly, the taxi driver knew all about Yusof and his work. Professor Profundo found that gratifying.

When they arrived at the kampong, it was quiet. The villagers were out, presumably working. There were a few women about, a few dogs, ducks, and chickens, cockerels in baskets, but otherwise nobody. The Professor asked an old woman for Yusof. She pointed to the large house at the end of the lane. But the house was empty. The Professor wandered on, through the vegetable and fruit gardens, looking carefully at the plants as he went. Periodically, he removed his white panama hat to fan himself. He carried a large red handkerchief with which he wiped the perspiration from his face. *'Oh dear, it is so very humid!'* He must ask Yusof how he managed to get these plants to fruit so well. And how did he manage to do it without insecticide? All very interesting! Toby, following in his wake, was intrigued. He had never been to Malagiar before.

Toby jumped, then started laughing. A small monkey, level with his face, had spat a fruit kernel straight into Toby's eye. Rubbing his eye, Toby grinned at the monkey, which scratched its head and grinned back.

They entered the animal enclosure. The Professor looked long and carefully at each of the residents. *'So this is what he's doing. Well done, Yusof. I can't wait to meet you again, old Pal.'*

"See here, Toby. He's healing these poor creatures with medicines from the forest. Isn't that wonderful."

They wandered on again, and found all Aishah's newly planted seedlings. The Professor got really excited.

"Toby, Toby! Just look at this. This is wonderful. Bending down, examining a young sapling, he did not notice the slim woman approaching.

"Can I help you?"

The Professor straightened. A little embarrassed at being found, effectively, in someone else's garden, his face went very red.

"So sorry, Ma'am. I'm looking for......"

"Professor, Professor Profundo, don't you recognise me? I can't believe it's you" Aishah cried happily.

"Oh My Dear, My Dear, it's Aishah, isn't it?"

"Yes, Professor, it's me. What are you doing here? This is such a nice surprise. Yusof will be back soon. Come up to the house." And she led the way back to the house, where they settled down on the verandah, talking non-stop.

"We've come to see Yusof, find out what's going on. This is my son, Toby. Of course, he was not born when last we met. Toby, say how d'ye do. Marjorie - you remember Marjorie, my wife, - sends her love."

"How do you do, Ma'am" said Toby, standing up.

"How do you do, Toby. What nice manners you have. Well, I have news for you too, Professor. Yusof and I have two children now, Ibrahim and Faradilla. They have gone swimming with their friends, but they will be back soon. Ibrahim is twelve, Toby, probably about your age, and Faradilla is six. Ah, I see Yusof approaching. He is carrying a basket full of plants, as usual." She laughed. "You will remember that, Professor. He still always carries plants wherever he goes. He will be so surprised and so pleased to see you."

"Abang, Abang" she called, leaning over the verandah. "We have visitors. A surprise." Yusof waved to her, increasing his pace.

When he saw the Professor, he strode straight towards him and gave him a bear-like hug. The Professor reciprocated. Standing back, they looked each other up and down.

"You have not changed, Professor" chuckled Yusof.

"Neither have you, apart from a few more grey hairs" retorted the Professor.

"I am so glad you came, Professor. We have a lot to talk about. You must stay with us tonight. I hope you have made no other arrangements."

"I was hoping you would say that. We would love to stay, wouldn't we, Toby."

The two men wandered off, arm in arm. Aishah busied herself about the house, and Toby, left to his own devices, went off to explore. A strange little dog followed him. It was Katak.

Returning from their swim, Ibrahim and Faradilla saw an unknown white boy playing with Katak. They introduced themselves. He said his name was Toby, and that his Dad was visiting Yusof, and that, actually, they would be staying the night with Yusof and his family.

"But that's us" cried Ibrahim delightedly. "Come on. You can help us feed the animals"

They got on really well. Toby was good at handling the hurt creatures and, in no time at all, they had finished their chores.

That evening, over dinner, Yusof and Ibrahim explained to the Professor all that had been happening. The Professor and Toby listened intently.

"Well, I must say! What an adventure! I do wish we had got here sooner. We've missed all the fun. And I cannot believe that you got the Orang Asli and the creatures to co-operate with you. It's because Toby received one of the children's e.mails, of course, that we are here. I felt it might be a nice little problem to solve. I did not know you were already on to it" Professor Profundo chuckled. He liked problems.

"The whole thing was the children's doing." Yusof explained. "Ibrahim's friend, Joseph, started it all. They organised everything. I do not believe that anyone else could have achieved what the children did."

Professor Profundo and Toby looked at Ibrahim with admiration. Ibrahim squirmed a little. He was embarrassed at this attention.

"You will meet the other children tomorrow. They always come early to help with the animals."

"Tomorrow is a new day" said the Professor, standing up and stretching. "Now, if you do not mind, I am very tired, and would like to go to bed. Today has already been quite an adventure, you know."

CHAPTER

When Vinod arrived at the kampong in the morning, he proudly announced:

"I have a new baby brother now. He was born last night, and Papa says I have a new responsibility, to look after him."

"Congratulations" said Joseph.

"That is very nice" said Ibrahim.

"Is he all shrivelled, like a pickled plum?" asked Xin Hui, who did not really know much about babies.

"I think monkeys are much prettier when they are born. Babies look like pigs. But I expect he will be handsome when he grows up" said Faradilla.

"He does look like a pickled plum, and he cries a lot." said Vinod.

Ibrahim introduced them to Toby, and they all started work. They had established a routine by now, and finished quickly.

"Some of these animals are recovering, but others are too badly hurt or burned to be able to go back to the wild again, so we shall have to keep them here for ever, or else build another safe place for them" explained Ibrahim. "Bapa is worried about what we should do if the kampong is burned down."

"Just wait and see" said Toby. "My Dad has a lot of influence in his own way. He will help."

"We should go and check the fire break" said Joseph. "The evil palm oil baron's men will try to fire the forest soon."

The children took Toby into the forest, showed him the fire break they had dug. It was still dry. They hoped it would rain soon, so that it would fill up with water. Digging it had been a mammoth task. Toby was suitably impressed.

"The creatures really helped you? And the Orang Asli? Gosh, I wish I had been there. And you got all the grown-ups to help? Oh Boy!"

Toby was a little envious of the children. He would have given anything to be with them. Toby was enchanted by the forest. Everywhere he looked there was movement, life, light and shade. He knew they were being watched, but he did not feel uncomfortable.

They heard a soft rustling in the treetop overhead. Looking up, they saw a huge orang utan.

"Tunku" the other children cried. Tunku abseiled down to meet them. He had been out and about, patrolling the forest, gleaning what information he could. Toby could hardly believe his eyes. Tunku and Ibrahim spent several minutes together, communicating. Ibrahim looked troubled.

"What is it?" asked Joseph.

"The rangers have been keeping tabs on the evil palm oil baron's men. They are going to fire the forest tomorrow. They do not know that we have dug the fire break, but, as there is no water in it, Matahari and Tunku believe the flames will leap across it quite easily. They say it is because of the direction of the wind. The wind will carry the flames deep into the forest."

The children were silent, wrestling with this terrible thought that, after all their efforts, they were still helpless in the face of the evil palm oil baron's men.

"The trouble is we cannot get the grown-ups to help. They are all at work. I wish it would rain. I think that Ibrahim, Vinod and I should go, do as much as we can to stop them, and Toby too, if he wants to. Xin Hui and Faradilla are too little." Joseph was thinking out loud.

"I'm coming too. You cannot stop me, lah." chipped in Xin Hui indignantly.

"And me" said Faradilla.

"But it is going to be dangerous. You could get burned," said Ibrahim.

"I have an idea" said Joseph. "Have you got the telephone number of that reporter, what's her name, Shirley Pooper? I shall telephone her, get her down here. She will do anything for a good story. The plan is this: we will line up along the road, facing them, with our backs to the forest. Shirley Pooper will be there with Bert, taking lots of photographs, as we face up to the evil palm oil baron's men. They will not dare attack us or fire the forest with a reporter there recording everything they do. After all, we are only children."

Vinod laughed, delighted with the plan.

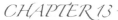

"That will do for one day, but what about the next day and the day after that, and the....."

Xin Hui was being practical again.

Joseph felt weighted down by responsibility. "I do not know, Xin Hui. But it might buy us time to think and plan something else."

Tunku and Ibrahim were talking to each other again, then Tunku, waving farewell, glided off into the trees.

"We must go and speak to my father" said Ibrahim.

"And mine. He will definitely want to know about this." said Toby.

⋘∘⋙∘⋘∘⋙∘⋘∘⋙∘⋘∘⋙∘⋘

In the shabby offices of the South East Asia Gazette, Shirley Pooper was having a blazing row with her boss, Sam, the editor. She had written the best piece of her life, and she knew it. But Sam was adamant.

"Shirley. We cannot go to print with this. The palm oil baron is the most powerful man in the country. You are accusing him of bribery and corruption without evidence. You have to have strong evidence to go to print. He will sue us, sue you, and within twenty-four hours we will be out of business."

"But, Sam, it's a scoop. The best!"

"Watch my lips, Shirley. Without evidence it is nothing. Evidence! Evidence! Evidence! Get the evidence." He stormed out of the office, slamming the door behind him. Shirley was right. It was a good scoop, but he did not dare go to print. If she could get evidence-that would be something else!

Then the 'phone rang. "I'd like to speak to Shirley Pooper, please." It was Joseph. He explained what he wanted. Shirley's heart was racing. *These kids are on to something. Maybe! Just maybe I'll get that evidence, or something anyway'* She listened, as Joseph gave instructions.

"We'll be there" she said "You can depend on us". *'I bet I can!'* thought Joseph.

The children were sitting on the anjung with Yusof and Professor Profundo. They explained what Tunku had told them, and their plan of action. Joseph said Shirley had committed to being there as well.

"My Dears, we shall certainly join you" said Professor Profundo, "won't we, Yusof. Why, I would not miss this for anything. Meantime, I have one or two people to see this afternoon." He sounded mysterious. The children did not like to question him. Toby, though, knew he was up to something.

"You are quite right, Professor," Yusof answered. "We shall be there, Joseph. But these men are determined. It may be dangerous. I am not sure about the girls..."

"We are going, Ayah. Nothing will stop us." said Faradilla firmly.

Early the next morning, the children, the Professor and Yusof were waiting beside the dirt track when the evil palm oil baron's men arrived. Casually, the men climbed off the back of the lorry. They were surprised to find children here, but got on with the task of pulling firing equipment off the lorry. Suddenly, Faradilla and Xin Hui were standing, determined, defiant, in front of them. The girls were holding hands tightly.

"We will not allow you to fire the forest" said Xin Hui. Faradilla nodded her head firmly in agreement. The boys moved up, behind the girls.

"No, we will not." said Joseph.

"What? What is this?" asked Ah Kong, laughing. "Since when have we taken orders from children? Get out of our way, children. You will get hurt." He went to push past them. The Professor emerged from the undergrowth.

"My dear fellow, you had better listen to these children. This forest is a national treasure, you know – priceless, quite priceless! It is worth millions and millions of dollars."

Yusof was behind the professor. He nodded in agreement. Ah Kong hesitated. This was unexpected. How many more of these people were there?

"I have got my orders" he growled, pushing past Xin Hui and Faradilla. We are firing the forest today, now!"

"Oh no, you don't" Joseph was in front of him. "And leave those girls alone. Don't you dare push them."

Ibrahim, Vinod and Toby stood alongside Joseph. Whichever way Ah Kong tried to turn, the children were there in front of him. Ah Kong yelled at his men to get on with it. He was very angry that he had lost face. Yusof, the Professor, and the boys quietly moved in front of, but at just more than arm's length from, any man who tried to fulfil his orders. The girls remained firmly planted in front of Ah Kong. He moved to the left, they moved to the left. He moved to the right, they moved to the right. He raised his arm to lash out and, in doing so, saw Bert, a few metres away, filming everything. And he saw Shirley, talking rapidly into a dictaphone. He recognised her. She was the reporter who had upset the palm oil baron a couple of days previously. He had had enough. Cursing, he called his men, telling them to get back in to the lorry.

"We shall be back" he growled, as they drove off.

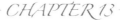

Toby was ecstatic. "We've won!" he shouted, jumping up and down.

"Only the first bout," said Joseph, "They will be back."

Xin Hui and Faradilla were trembling, now that it was all over.

"You were both very brave," said Yusof kindly.

Shirley came running up. "We got it, we got it all on film," she cried.

Yusof shook his head sorrowfully. "I am afraid a lot more is to come. The evil palm oil baron will be very angry, and he will not give up. I shall go now and speak to the Orang Asli. We shall need their help."

"I am coming with you," cried the Professor, determined not to be left out of this. He had always wanted to get to know the Orang Asli. They had so much knowledge about the plants and their properties, knowledge the professor would give his eye teeth to have. Yusof smiled. "Of course you are, Professor."

The children sank down on the grass with Shirley and Bert. They agreed that the evil palm oil baron's men would be back the next day with much greater force. They needed a plan of action, and it was important that Shirley and Bert should film everything, but they were to keep it absolutely to themselves, tell no-one, until after everything was over. Shirley and Bert were delighted. This would be a scoop for both of them. She would get a great story, and he would get great photographs. Little did he know just how great his photographs would prove to be.

Ibrahim called into the forest. "We need to tell Tunku," he explained. Within seconds Tunku was swinging effortlessly towards them. Shirley's heart stopped. He was enormous.

CHAPTER 13

Bert fumbled for his camera, not quite believing his own eyes. Tunku dropped down beside them, draping his long, hairy arm over Ibrahim's small shoulders. Bert got his shot.

"Tunku, it's bad news." Ibrahim explained "You have to get all the creatures deep, deep into the forest. They must start off right away, otherwise they may be burned tomorrow. We are going to try and hold off the evil palm oil baron's men, but we do not have much hope that we shall succeed. There will be many of them."

"We shall try, Tunku. We shall try with all our might." said Joseph." We shall not allow them to burn your forest."

"You see, it's our forest too!" said Faradilla.

The children devised a plan. Tunku looked gravely from one young face to another. He looked at Shirley and at Bert. Delicately, with his long, strong fingers, he reached out and touched Shirley's arm. She was thrilled. Never in all her life had she experienced anything like this. As soon as he knew their plan of action, Tunku took his leave. He had a lot to do. So had the children.

Shirley and Bert returned to the offices of the South East Asia Gazette. She had a story to write. He had photographs to develop. Sam, the boss, wondered what they were up to, but they were working with such intensity, he thought it best not to interrupt.

The children spent the whole afternoon gathering bucketfuls of water, and depositing them at even intervals along the firebreak. *'They are such small buckets. I don't suppose they will do much good. But, as Mum says, better something than nothing.'* Joseph was far more worried than he admitted to the others. This was going to be an enormous task.

Shirley Pooper and Bert

CHAPTER 14

The children knew approximately where the evil palm oil baron's men would pull up their lorries to unload. Following their plan, the boys pushed and shoved the two girls up into a tree, where they made themselves comfortable, sitting in a crook in the branches. They had a good view of the road from up there. Nervous and tense, the four boys stationed themselves at ten yard intervals along the road, and waited. Well hidden in the undergrowth, they were each armed with a catapult and a supply of small pebbles. The girls had catapults and pebbles too, but Joseph did not think they would be able to use them.

There was a commotion on the road. Shirley and Bert had arrived, riding bicycles. They were hiding their bicycles in bushes when Bert slipped on an incline. His cameras tumbled down the slope. Bert swore and scrambled down the slope to retrieve them whilst Shirley was calling encouragement.

Joseph and Toby came out of hiding.

"Oh, there you are" Shirley called, waving her arm excitedly.

Joseph ran to her. "Shush, Shirley" Joseph said "We don't know how close any of the men might be. They could be here already." Ibrahim and Vinod, standing on tiptoe, could just see what was going on.

"Sorry" Shirley whispered. Bert emerged from the ditch he had climbed into, looking pained, but at least he had all his cameras. They agreed that Shirley, like the girls, could see everything much better from high up in the branches of a tree. With a bit of pushing and shoving, they got her up. She broke a couple of her vermilion coloured nails. *'What the heck! This is more interesting than nails. My scoop!'* Bert would not be persuaded to climb a tree. "No, my place is here, on the ground. I need to get to the action." But he did agree to hide himself, at least initially.

They did not have to wait long. Three beaten up lorries came into sight. They stopped, and started to unload. Ah Kong was there, shouting grimly at the men. He was not in a frame of mind to put up with any nonsense today. Besides, if they did not fire the forest today, the palm oil baron would find out, and it was more than his job was worth to upset the palm oil baron.

There was a soft fizz of air, and a small pebble hit Ah Kong just behind the ear. "Ow" he reached up his hand and rubbed the spot. It was wet. He withdrew his hand. Blood! One of the men yowled as another small pebble caught him on the cheekbone. *'That was a good one!'* Toby was enjoying himself. Every time one of the men moved, a pebble came flying out from the forest. The children had been practicing. They were sparing with the pebbles, making them last, so each one had to find its mark. *'Those children! They are here again. I thought I had frightened them off yesterday. Well, today we'll teach them a lesson they won't forget.'* Angrily, Ah Kong retreated behind one of the lorries. He was making a 'phone call. Then he called to his men. They all climbed back into the lorries. Joseph held his breath. *They cannot possibly be giving up already.'* The men sat in their lorries, doing nothing, for twenty minutes. The children did not dare move.

Shirley, from her vantage point, was the first to spot the convoy of lorries heading towards them. Ah Kong had called up reinforcements.' *Joseph, Joseph, how am I to tell Joseph'?*But she need not have worried. An unseen Siamang boomed a warning. Xin Hui and Faradilla were next to spot the lorries. The boys, on the ground, had not seen them yet, but Xin Hui hissed a warning to Vinod, who was the nearest to her, and he passed it on to Ibrahim, who, in turn, passed it on to Toby and Joseph. They waited.

'Oh no!' At least thirty more lorries arrived, all full of men and equipment. *'This is getting serious. The girls!'* Joseph looked across at the girls up in the tree. They seemed quite happy. Faradilla was watching the men intently with her big, unblinking eyes. *'She's like a little cat up there.'* Xin Hui was watching them too, catapult raised, ready to strike. He could just make out Vinod and Ibrahim, crouching behind bushes, concentrating, poised for action. And then there was Toby. He had taken a liking to Toby, although he scarcely knew him. Big, strong, and open, Toby was proving to be a major asset. They watched, and waited. The suspense was tangible. Even the forest was silent, sensing the threat.

Once the lorries had parked, men erupted from them all at the same time, bringing equipment: torches, flame throwers, clubs, cutters, and knives. The children were aiming their pebbles well. They could tell from the yowls emitting spasmodically from the direction of the lorries. But there must have been about three hundred men, and only six children. Some of the men approached the edge of the forest; they set about laying out their equipment. Other men stood guard over them, clubs, torches, and shovels in their hands. It looked serious. If they should start a fire now, the children were caught directly in its path. The boys could run, but what about the girls up in the tree?

They were outnumbered. Joseph was considering whether they should pull back. They had a pre-arranged signal. When he gave it, they would all fall back to the fire-break. It would mean the girls would have to come down to ground level – not so safe. He was just about to give the signal when something whooshed through the air, over his head. He looked up. The trees above were full of macaques, gibbons, proboscis, all manner of monkeys. And they were throwing fruit, nuts, twigs, anything they could get their hands on, at the men. The children were delighted and heartened to see them. The 'whoosh' had been a large, ripe mango. It caught Ah Kong squarely on the side of his head, splitting the skin of the fruit which slithered in a sticky, gooey mess down Ah Kong's back, inside his shirt. He tried to scoop the fruit out of his shirt, but could not reach. Within minutes, the sweet smell and sticky flesh had attracted swarms of flies. Ah Kong waved his arms about, to no avail. The flies massed around his head. He shouted. The men rushed forward. They were in attack mode. The children raised their catapults, hurling pebbles with all their might. The monkeys chucked down anything and everything they could get their hands on. But the men kept coming. The girls had slithered down the tree by now. Together with the boys, they retreated, one step at a time, still hurling pebbles.

A snake slithered through Ibrahim's legs. He hardly noticed it, but it got one of the men, wrapping itself around his leg. The man screamed, thrashing about in the undergrowth. He went down. The monkeys were making a lot of noise now. The men were shouting. And still the missiles kept coming. Joseph, looking behind him for a moment, spotted Orang Asli with their blow-pipes, and bows and arrows. Further into the forest, Faradilla and Xin Hui shinned up another tree. Faradilla was pleased to see Tunku's Number One Son up there, hurling large, smelly, ripe durians at the men. He had a good aim. Faradilla smiled, and tapped Xin Hui on the shoulder, indicating Number One Son. Xin Hui laughed, and renewed her efforts with the catapult.

The men kept coming. They were trying to torch the undergrowth, which was now alive with creatures, all determined to save their forest. One young fellow got stung on the ankle by a scorpion. A few more found themselves covered in large ants. Their bites were particularly painful. The small creatures on the ground were all there, helping the children, sacrificing themselves for their beloved forest. The Orang Asli were blowing little darts from their blow pipes. They were not poisoned, but they still hurt. Some of the men managed to start a fire. Joseph and Ibrahim rushed over and frantically tried to beat out the flames. More men were starting another fire further down the line. Toby and Vinod tackled that one. And then another started, and another. Their task was impossible.

The earth trembled. They all felt it. A mighty trumpeting shook the very ground they stood on, and Matahari and Ribut, and several other elephants, among them Halilintar and Bijaksana whom Joseph and Ibrahim had met briefly at the Grand Convention, burst out of the forest. Without hesitating, they charged straight towards the lorries. They butted them, pushed them over, squashed them. They instilled fear in the hearts of the evil men who now had no escape route. Turning, ears flapping, the elephants charged at the small groups of men, who scattered in disarray. The children and Shirley, who had shinned down her tree, busied themselves putting out the fires whilst the men were occupied by the elephants. Bert, not believing his luck, and oblivious of any danger, was running round clicking away with his camera.

They had forgotten Ah Kong. He had called for more reinforcements. More lorries arrived. This time, the men had guns. Joseph spotted them as they arrived. He saw the guns.

"They have got guns!" he screamed at anyone who could hear. "They've got guns!" Bert ran up to him, puffing,

"They won't shoot" he puffed, "You're children. They won't shoot at children."

More fires were being lit even as they spoke. A shot rang out. A bullet passed by Bert's nose, about an inch away. "Take cover!" he yelled, pulling at Joseph as he dived to the ground.

Shirley Pooper, Faradilla and Xin Hui had been so preoccupied putting out a fire, they had not noticed that other fires had crept up all around them. They were surrounded. "How do we get out?" shouted Xin Hui. Faradilla looked around, frantically trying to find an opening. Shirley screamed. A great grey form hurtled towards them through the fires."Moonlight" Xin Hui squealed. "It's Moonlight". Cahaya Bulan, hardly pausing in her stride, scooped Xin Hui up with her trunk, depositing the child on her back, then Faradilla, and, finally Shirley Pooper. With the three girls, and out of kindness we include Shirley Pooper in this description, clinging on, she made off, through the fire, towards the fire-break deeper in the forest. The big male elephants were busy, chasing the men off, stamping out the fires, blowing dust on them.

Ibrahim and Vinod had also found themselves trapped by the fires. Suddenly Tunku was hurling himself through the trees, charging to their rescue. He indicated to Ibrahim, who climbed on his back and shouted at Vinod to do the same. With the two boys clinging on, Tunku, wasting no time, leaped up, above the flames, and, propelling himself from branch to branch, carried them safely back towards the fire break, where he set them down. "Whew!" breathed Vinod. "That was something!"

In the meantime, the Orang Asli with their blow pipes had been out-manoeuvred by the men with guns. They had

also retreated to the fire-break. Bert, pulling Joseph up by the collar of his shirt, cried "Run. Run for cover!" They ran, stumbled, fell, picked themselves up, continued. Bert was dragged down by his cameras. "Give me one of those," shouted Joseph. Bert handed one across to Joseph. It made the running easier. Behind them, Joseph could hear the men shouting, he could hear the "whoosh" as flames caught trees, and he could hear the rumbling and trumpeting of the elephants. There were shots.

"Toby. Where's Toby? Has anyone seen Toby?" The last Joseph had seen of Toby, he had been running towards some of Ah Kong's equipment. Where was he now? Panic welled up inside Joseph.

"I'll have to go back and find him" he said to Ibrahim.

"I am coming with you" said Ibrahim.

"No you are not. You need to be here. You have to look after the others. You're the next oldest."

With that, Joseph set off, back towards the evil palm oil baron's men, their fire raising equipment, their guns, and their broken lorries. He was relieved to see that the elephants were still ransacking everything, keeping the men on the move, never letting them rest. Shots were being fired, but they were wild shots. None of the men had time to stop and take aim. *'If this were not real, it would be really funny.'* Joseph thought as he watched an elephant - it was Bijaksana, trunk raised in indignation, ears flapping wide, tail raised, chasing half a dozen men who, in sheer panic, threw down their weapons and fled as fast as their legs would carry them. Bijaksana chased them into a big ditch. But the funniest thing was that the ditch was already full of men, and standing round the top edge were Matahari, rumbling loudly, Ribut, and Halilintar. The men were on their knees, or sitting. They were all shaking. Every time one of them moved, Matahari moved menacingly towards him, rumbling loudly, head down, ears flapping widely. Joseph chuckled. He knew the elephants would not harm them. He heard movement behind. Turning quickly, he saw Bert emerge, camera to his eye, clicking as if his life depended on it. He was taking shots of the elephants round the ditch, with men in the bottom. Strangely for a human, he had never shown any fear of the creatures, even when they were being fierce.

Near the broken lorries, Joseph saw Ah Kong and a few other men. They were gathering up what remained of their firing equipment. A lot of it looked broken – no doubt trampled by the elephants. Then he spotted Toby, very close to the men, crouching down behind a lorry. Soon, the men had gathered up all they could, and made their way off, up the road, on foot. The elephants round the ditch moved to the far side, so that the men there could scramble out, and join their mates. The elephants followed them. The men ran as fast as they could. Once they got to the road, they kept on running. The others, already there, seeing the elephants, started running as well. They kept on running until they disappeared over the horizon.

Toby joined Joseph.

"I wanted to hear what they were saying" he said. "It was interesting. But at least we know what they are going to do."

"What's that?" asked Joseph.

"I am so tired. Can we talk about it later. We have got a little time, you know, before they do any more." Toby looked exhausted. Joseph recalled that he had only arrived in the country a couple of days ago, and was not yet accustomed to the heat and the humidity.

CHAPTER *15*

Professor Profundo was having tea at Government House with the Prime Minister. They had not seen each other for a couple of years and, although not as great a friend of the Prime Minister as he was of Yusof, the Professor was pleased to be seeing him again. And the Prime Minister was pleased to see the Professor. He rather liked this eccentric Englishman who was so knowledgeable about all sorts of interesting things.

"My Dear Professor" he said, standing as the Professor entered the room. He advanced to greet him, shaking him heartily by the hand.

"My Dear Prime Minister" returned the Professor with a big smile. "You have not changed at all. Just the same old Teo."

"Unfortunately, I have had to change, and not, I think, for the better."

And so the two gentlemen took tea, reminiscing fondly, exchanging news and views, updating themselves, each on the other's experiences.

"And what are you up to now, Professor? What brings you to Malagiar?" the Prime Minister asked him kindly.

"Well, Teo, you know how passionate I am about my plants. I thought it was time I looked up my old friend, Yusof. You remember Yusof? And, of course, what I really want is to find and study the Rafflesia. Yusof will help me. But Yusof, too, is doing some fascinating research, and I want to spend some time with him. We did work together in the past, you know – very successfully, as it happens, although I cannot remember what it was we worked on."

"Ah yes, the Rafflesia." The Prime Minister clearly had no clue as to what the Professor was talking about.

"You must know the Rafflesia, Prime Minister. It is the world's largest plant. Why, some flowers are about a metre across. Fascinating plant. Quite fascinating!"

"Yes, of course. But you must remember, Professor, that plants are not quite my thing."

"That brings me to what I want to talk to you about, Prime Minister." The Prime Minister looked at him quizzically. "Are you aware to what degree the forests are being destroyed in this country? Are you aware of the harm and damage being done to your own environment? Are you aware that people out there are destroying your own ecology for generations to come, perhaps for ever?"

"Well, that is rather strong, Professor. After all, by your own admission, you have only been here for a couple of days."

"Teo, it is largely what brought me here. I remember now. You know I have a tendency to be absent-minded. I forget things, but only temporarily. I am quite serious. What is happening to your country is serious. Why, you can drive for five hundred miles and there is nothing as far as the eye can see but Palm Oil Trees, thousands and thousands of Palm Oil Trees."

"Palm Oil brings us revenue, Professor. We need that income stream very badly."

"Consider the price you are paying. There are no more kampongs, no more paddy fields, no more rubber plantations, tin mines, tea plantations. There is no room left to grow food, crops and livestock. It has all been sacrificed for palm oil. And the people are having to live in hideous high rise apartment blocks. These are country people, men and women of the soil. They love their land, their buffalo, their chickens, their fighting cockerels. When they had these things the people were largely self-sufficient, but now they are wholly dependent on imported foods."

"Compared with the western world, we were a backward nation, Professor. Change has to take place. Our way of life has had to change."

"Can you honestly tell me you believe it is for the better? These gentle people, your people, do not even have a small garden of their own. What can be better than growing your own food, self-sufficiency? What is wrong with simplicity? What sort of a life style have they now, cooped up in small apartments, high up in the sky, excommunicated from the realities of life, with nothing to do but watch television, shop, eat and drink? You cannot tell me that is better. What you are doing will cause great unhappiness, mental illness, suicides even. Is that what you want for your people?"

"It is better for the country, Professor. I do believe that you exaggerate."

"You mean it makes more money for the government, and gives it more control over the people." The Professor was enjoying himself now. He was having a field day.

"I would not allow anyone else to speak to me like this, Professor. I do not like it."

The Professor smiled roundly "I know. That is why it is so important for me to speak my mind. If I do not, who else will?"

"Teo, are you aware that one of your palm oil barons is, at any moment, about to burn down another five hundred thousand hectares of prime forest. This is forest, Teo, which is priceless. It is thousands of years old. There are so many secrets for survival in that forest. Even now, Yusof is liaising with the Orang Asli, researching the medicinal qualities of many of the plants. Did you know that the Orang Asli have never, ever suffered from Dengue fever? Not one of them. They use a plant from the forest as a preventative. Just think what knowledge we could extract from these people, what benefits we could gain from these plants. Instead, you are burning them all down to plant palm oil." The Professor made his disgust quite clear. "And, incidentally, what do you intend to do about the Orang Asli. How will they fare if forced out of the forest? Not to speak of the creatures who live there and enrich our planet, our experience of life. What about your national heritage?"

"I have given Universal Palm Oil Inc. the right to replant five hundred thousand hectares of forest, yes. This is necessary. We need more palm oil to provide the revenue to pay for our armed forces, and for our development."

"What development? My own view is that you are destroying your once beautiful and rich country. Instead of self-sufficiency, you now rely on imports. Your people are unhappy. You choose to ignore that. And why do you need to spend so much on armed forces? You are not under any threat. Teo, you and I have been friends for a long time, but you are right, you have changed. And I do not like what you are doing to your country."

"The palm oil baron is a very good friend of mine, Professor." He stood up. Unfortunately, I have another engagement now. Perhaps we might continue our discussion another day."

Rising, the Professor sighed.

"Teo, we have known each other for a long time. I do not want us to become enemies, but something has to be done. I **will** be in touch again."

They shook hands, and the Professor went on his way. He was saddened. He felt that somewhere along the way Teo had lost touch. He had lost compassion, consideration for others, the concept of living in harmony with nature. He had hardened. All he seemed to be interested in was money. Could he, the Professor, help him to find these important principles of life again? He was an old and dear friend, after all.

꧁꧂꧁꧂꧁꧂꧁꧂꧁꧂

Joseph and Toby looked around them. There were still a few smoking patches of ground, but, by and large, the fires had been put out before they had time to take a hold. Bert had stopped taking photographs. He headed towards them.

"What now, Joseph?" he asked.

"I think we had better get back to the others. They will be wondering what is happening."

They set off, slowly, wearily, towards the fire break, arriving without incident. The other children, Shirley Pooper, and some of the Orang Asli were there, squatting on the ground. The children were exhausted. The elephants, Tunku, the monkeys, had all disappeared as quickly and quietly as they had arrived. What Joseph found most amazing was the way in which the elephants, big creatures as they were, could move so silently through the forest.

Ibrahim was talking to an elder of the Orang Asli.

"I told him they will probably be back tomorrow. He says the Orang Asli will fight to the last to save their forest." He smiled at the swarthy little man. "So will I".

"I think we all will" said Joseph.

The Orang Asli had already melted into the forest. It was a little unnerving, the way they moved so quietly, like the animals. Shirley and Bert headed off. Shirley's head was spinning with the story she was going to write, and Bert was anxious to get back to his laboratory where he could develop the photographs he had taken.

⚬⚬⚬⚬⚬⚬⚬⚬⚬

On the way home, the children talked, but not much. Tomorrow would be an even harder day. They were not sure how they would cope.

"We only won today because Matahari and his tribe came to help," said Ibrahim.

"Yes, Moonlight saved Faradilla and me. Otherwise we would have been burned. Eeeh, I do love Moonlight. And tomorrow the evil palm oil baron's men will bring even more reinforcements, lah! "

"Tunku was the greatest" said Vinod, still ecstatic about his flight through the trees.

Joseph was anxious. "What did you hear, Toby?"

"Well, that supervisor fellow is really angry. They will not come back again this week, but will come next week, when they have had time to get some more equipment. From what he was saying, I think they are going to bring in long distance flame throwers and a lot more men. Honestly, Joseph, I think they will stop at nothing."

Joseph was worried, but relieved at the same time.

"Well, that gives us a little time. I do wish it would rain. It has not rained for weeks. If only it would rain!"

Little Faradilla was limping heavily, and her arm was scratched. Joseph stopped her and told her to get on his back. He would give her a piggy-back. She accepted gratefully.

Ibrahim chipped in

"Cheer up. Joseph, we have kept them off so far, and I know that Bapa and the Professor are doing everything they can to help. I am hungry. I hope Ibu will have food waiting for us."

The children quickened their pace. Vinod suddenly disappeared. They heard him yowl; it came from down below. Looking down, they saw a hole in the undergrowth. Underneath was a great pit.

"Hey, Vinod! Are you O.K.?" shouted Joseph, quickly easing Faradilla off his back. She crawled on all fours to the edge of the pit and peered down. She could hear Vinod moaning.

"He's hurt" said Faradilla. "I can see him. He is all crumpled up in the corner. There are lots of bugs in there."

"Vinod, Vinod!" Joseph, Ibrahim and Toby clustered around the edge of the pit. Ibrahim held Xin Hui back.

"No Xin Hui, it is too dangerous. Faradilla, get back! You'll fall in too. Vinod, are you alright? Answer us, Vinod." There was no response.

"I think he's concussed. We shall have to get him out somehow." The children looked helplessly at each other.

"Take off your tee-shirts. They're all covered in smoke and soot anyway." said Xin Hui. The three boys did as they were told. "We'll have to tie them together and make a rope ladder out of the tee shirts. One of us will have to go down. Faradilla is too small but, apart from her, I am the lightest, so I should go."

"I have got a better idea." said Ibrahim. He ran over to a thicket of trees and pulled down a couple of long lianas. "These will be better." He quickly wound one of the lianas round the trunk of a sturdy tree, and fed the length of it out towards the pit. Then he attached both ends of the second liana to the first, creating a large loop. "There. That will be better."

Xin Hui tied it round herself, using the tee-shirts as padding so that the liana did not cut into her, and gingerly started abseiling backwards down the wall of the pit. It smelled funny down here, damp and musty. There had not been any rain for weeks. The forest above was tinder dry, but down here the earth was definitely not dried out. There were ferns growing out of the walls of the pit, which she was able to grab on to, and lots of creepy crawlies. Xin Hui shuddered. When she got to the bottom she called out to the others to tell them she was safely on the bottom. The floor of the pit was soft and spongy. There was a lot of dead, rotting vegetation down there. *'At least Vinod had a soft fall'* she thought. She could just make out Vinod's form, huddled in the corner. Going over to him she touched him on the arm, shook him gently.

"Vinod! Vinod! Can you hear me? Are you still alive?" He stirred, and mumbled, but she could not understand what he was saying.

"I shall tie the liana around him, and you will have to pull him up" she called. "I shall wait here, and then you can drop the liana back down for me."

Joseph, Ibrahim and Toby lined up, grabbing hold of the liana. When Xin Hui shouted, they started to pull. Vinod was heavier than he looked. They struggled.

"Pull! Pull! Pull!" chanted Faradilla at the top of the pit, and Xin Hui on the bottom, in unison. Gradually Vinod was hauled up, his body bumping against the sides of the pit as he lurched upwards. Xin Hui stood below him with arms outstretched (in case he should fall). Faradilla, at the top, ran and grabbed hold of the liana too. She pulled with all her might, helping the boys. Then, as if he had popped out of a bottle, Vinod was lying on the ground at the top of the pit. He was tossing and turning and mumbling. But he did not respond to the children's questions.

"I do not think he has any broken bones." said Ibrahim. "He is moving too easily. But how are we going to get him home? We shall have to carry him. We'll have to tie some planks together and pull him along on top of them."

"Hey! Hey! What about me, lah?" shouted Xin Hui. They had forgotten her. They did not hear. She shouted as loud as she could "Hey! Get me out of here. This is not funny, lah! Get me out."

Toby heard a rustling behind him. He looked over his shoulder and drew in his breath. A black bear with a yellow moon on its chest was standing upright on its hind legs, behind him. Ignoring the children, the bear made straight for the pit. Lying down at the edge, he swung one of his big paws down. Xin Hui was, at first, frightened, but then she just knew that the bear meant to help her. She reached our her hand, and was just able to grasp the bear's big paw. *'My goodness, what big claws!'* The bear pulled her easily to the top of the pit. The others gathered round.

"Xin Hui, are you alright?" "Gosh, Xin Hui, we had forgotten you." "Sorry, Xin Hui." they chorused.

Xin Hui's pride was damaged, but nothing else. She was not hurt. She had a little sulk, and then she felt better.

Ibrahim spoke to the bear. "It's alright" he said "Hitam Malam will carry Vinod and Faradilla on his back. He will come with us as far as the kampong."

With a lot of heaving and pulling, huffing and puffing, they managed to ease Vinod across the bear's back. Then Faradilla climbed up behind Vinod. Hitam Malam's back was very broad; Faradilla's little legs stuck out straight on either side, and she clung on to Vinod with one hand, and to the bear's fur with the other. They set off at a rolling gait, the other children following behind. The bear seemed to know its way. Without hesitation, it padded softly along trails unseen and unnoticed by humans. It pushed its way through dense, dark and shady undergrowth, smelling of damp earth, rotting vegetation and wood. Insects rustled constantly all around them. The cicadas were already singing again. It was getting darker in the forest. The crickets were starting their night chorus.

'Gosh, the sun is going down already. We have been in the forest all day.' thought Joseph. By time they reached the kampong, the children were so tired, they were staggering. Hitam Malam deposited Vinod and Faradilla safely on the anjung of Yusof's house. Katak was dancing around him, barking furiously, but the bear ignored him. He nuzzled Ibrahim, and made his way back into the forest.

"Oh, what a nice bear" said Xin Hui, "I do love all the animals, and especially Hitam Malam and Cahaya Bulan". Faradilla smiled and squeezed her hand "So do I." she whispered "That is why we have got to save them."

Aishah emerged from the house. "Ibu, Vinod's been hurt. He fell into a pit. Is he alright?"

Aishah bent down to Vinod, felt his forehead, gently tested his limbs.

"Well, I can see a big bump here, on his forehead, so he is a little concussed, I expect. His thick hair will have saved him from a lot of damage. It would have had the same effect as a motor-bike helmet. He seems to be all in one piece. Nothing appears to be broken." She looked up

"You children are so dirty. Go and take showers. I shall bring you clean sarongs and tee shirts in a minute." She dismissed them, bending towards Vinod, cleaning his face and hands with a clean, damp cloth.

When the children came back from their shower, Aishah had set out a large meal of fried rice and eggs, and water melon to follow. Vinod was sitting up, looking a lot better. He looked a bit sheepish when he saw the others.

"I am very sorry for being so silly," he said.

"You were not silly, Vinod. Nobody would have seen that pit. It must be one that the Orang Asli dug in the old days, to catch bears. Bapa told me there were some around."

The children tucked into the food. They were ravenous. Vinod ate just as well as any of the others.

"Ibu, we have been fighting off the evil palm oil baron's men. They tried to set fire to the forest today."

"What, you fought them on your own? You must tell your father about this. It is too dangerous for you children to tackle grown men on your own," said Aishan, concerned.

"No, Ibu, the Orang Asli came to help us, and so did the animals. You should have seen the elephants pushing over all the lorries." Ibrahim chuckled.

"Yes, and then they drove all the evil palm oil baron's men into a big pit and stood over them, and would not let them out" laughed Faradilla. "Well, they did let them out in the end, and chased them up the road, away from the forest." All the children were laughing at this memory.

"Then Vinod fell into an old bear pit, and Xin Hui was very brave. She went down and got him out. Well, we all helped. But we forgot about Xin Hui, and a big bear came and pulled her out, and then he carried Vinod and me all the way home."

Aishah smiled. *'How is it that these children have such an affinity with the creatures of the forest? It will keep them safe always.'* "I think you had better tell your father all this when he comes home," she said.

The children opted to stay the night at the kampong. When Yusof returned, he found seven young bodies (six children and Katak) curled up on the anjung, all snoring gently. Aishah told him what they had done that day. She was proud of them.

"But this is serious," retaliated Yusof. "They will come back again, and again. I do not know how the children, or anyone else, can stop them. And it is getting more dangerous each time. I do not know how long the forest will survive, or even the kampong. That man is ruthless."

CHAPTER 16

Professor Profundo was talking to Yusof.

"I am to lecture the students at the University this evening" he said. "I shall be talking about the plants of the forest, the necessity of preserving them. Indeed, I shall be talking about the necessity of preserving everything in the forest! I would like you to come, Yusof, as my guest speaker. I know I am giving you little time to prepare, but, with your knowledge, and your passion, you do not need to prepare."

"My dear friend, I am not sure. Normally, I would accept immediately. The issues are so important. But the children had a bad experience yesterday, and I feel I should be here for them."

The Professor's bushy eyebrows rose, he opened his eyes wide in question. Yusof explained what had happened the previous day. He told the Professor about the fight with the evil palm oil baron's men, and that the men would return, reinforced, within a week. He felt that he, Yusof, should get involved, call on the Orang Asli for help, and the villagers –

again! He sighed heavily. "I do not know how long this will go on for. I do not know how effective we can be. I do not know how long we can hold out. It is all very depressing, Professor."

Pulling his hat off, the Professor scratched his head. He patted Yusof awkwardly on the shoulder.

"There, there, My Dear Fellow. We cannot have you getting depressed like this. Why don't you come, and bring the children with you. Perhaps they could say something about why they are trying to preserve the forest. Eh? What do you think of that?"

Yusof smiled. The Professor was incorrigible. But it might work. "I am not sure. I would have to ask their parents for permission. And the children themselves. They may not want to. It will be very frightening for them, standing in front of so many people."

" And that son of yours, Ibrahim, is so knowledgeable. I hope one day that he will become my prize student."

"Well, maybe the boys, but the girls are too young" said Yusof. "I shall speak to them. They will be here in a minute."

The children had risen late, eaten breakfast, and gone for a leisurely swim. When they returned Yusof told them of the Professor's idea. They discussed it. Joseph was not sure. He was very nervous of standing up in public, as he had already discovered when addressing the villagers. Ibrahim, Vinod and Toby were very keen to go. Xin Hui indignantly pointed out that she had no intention of being left out.

"After all, it was me who went down into the bear pit to rescue Vinod," she pointed out.

Faradilla grabbed hold of Xin Hui's hand. "I am coming too" she announced. So it was settled. The Professor rubbed his hands together gleefully.

"Aha! We are going to have fun tonight," he announced.

The children telephoned their parents, got their permission. Mrs Chan was a little anxious about Xin Hui, but when she realised she would be accompanied by Yusof and the eminent botany Professor, she was reassured. Joseph, Vinod, and Xin Hui rushed home to change into smarter clothes. Ibrahim, Faradilla and Toby remained at Yusof's house. Ibrahim put on a clean white loose suit of long sleeved shirt and trousers, and a small plain black cap. Aishah loved dressing Faradilla for special occasions. She put a little fuchsia silk sarong on her, and a matching exquisitely embroidered kebaya. It was rich with flowers and blossoms in deep purples, golds, pale pinks, and greens, which Aishah had lovingly embroidered herself. The outfit was completed with a purple and gold sash. She wove fresh frangipani into Faradilla's long black hair, which shone like jet when it was brushed. Yusof swallowed hard when he saw his children dressed in their best clothes. He was very proud of them. Toby appeared. He had changed into beige linen trousers, and a white linen shirt.

Joseph, Vinod and Xin Hui arrived. Both the boys wore long trousers, and clean white shirts. They looked very grown up. Xin Hui had chosen a rich lemon yellow skirt and a cream shirt. Her hair, long and black like Faradilla's, was tied back with a lemon yellow ribbon, matching her skirt.

"Children, you all look wonderful," Aishah cried. And the Professor blew his nose very noisily indeed.

"Come along now. We had better be on our way," he said gruffly. They all piled into Yusof's car. It was a bit of a tight squeeze, but they managed. When they arrived at the University, the Professor and Yusof were greeted warmly by the Chancellor, who showed them to the lecture hall. He was somewhat surprised to see the children there too, but the Professor assured him that they were vital to his lecture. The hall was already filling up with students. It was quite scary. The children looked around them wide-eyed. *'One day I shall be sitting here, listening to lectures on botany, or maybe medicine'* thought Ibrahim.

Chairs were found for the children on the dais at the front of the lecture hall. Two chairs, a table, and a big screen were already up there. There was a computer on the table, a bottle of water, and two glasses. Somebody thoughtfully brought another bottle of water, and six more glasses, for the children. They made their way towards the waiting chairs and sat down. They were very quiet, a little over-awed by the occasion. The hall was now virtually full of students. The Professor checked his watch. Looking at Yusof, he smiled and nodded. "Time to go," he said, and they mounted the dais. The Professor made his way to the front. The chattering started to die down. Still he waited, until absolute silence fell in the hall.

"Good evening, Ladies and Gentlemen," he boomed. " As some of you are aware, my name is Professor Profundo. For those of you who have not heard of me, I am considered to be a leading authority on plant life, its place in our modern rushed lives, and, above all, its place in our fragile society. My lecture this evening is, however, going to be a little unusual. I would like to introduce to you my eminent friend, Professor Yusof Suleiman, who is undoubtedly one of the world's leading pharmacognosists. That is, he studies and researches the medicinal qualities of plants in the forest."

Ibrahim swelled with pride. He knew his father was very good at his job, but did not know he was 'eminent', a very important man. Joseph knew Yusof was very clever and worked with plants to create medicines and healing, but he did not know he was a Professor, a Pharmacognosist, neither did Vinod or Xin Hui.

"I would also like to introduce you to some very special children."

Turning towards them, he gestured "Joseph, Ibrahim, Vinod, Xin Hui, Faradilla." Joseph stared fixedly at his shoes, Ibrahim looked proudly ahead, Vinod blushed but looked ahead, Xin Hui looked at her shoes too, and blushed, and Faradilla tucked her foot into the rung under the seat of her chair, blushed and squirmed with embarrassment. "Oh, and Toby too" said the Professor. Toby grinned. Accustomed to his father's lectures, he was less nervous than the others.

The Professor then went on to explain that it is essential to get the right balance between our new modern technological life and the existing planet with all its benefits and its glory. He explained that the right ecological balance is essential to life itself, that animals and plant species evolve, adapt, just as we do. He went on to tell the students that he was currently working on pitcher plants. "You know, they trap insects, reduce them to soup, and then drink the soup for sustenance." And that he had recently developed a particular interest in the Rafflesia plant.

"How many of you have seen a Rafflesia plant?" he asked. Only a couple of hands were raised. The Professor nodded. "It is found deep in the forest and is very difficult to find until it actually flowers." The Professor was clicking on to slides on his computer as he spoke. Pictures and diagrams were coming up on the screen. The children were entranced. It lives most of its life underground, sucking off the root system of other plants. It is a parasite. When it flowers, it is only for a few days, but it is the largest flower in the world, bright red with a span frequently up to a metre across. There are twelve different varieties." He showed a slide of a huge red flower. "Isn't that marvellous, a miracle of nature!" he said, beaming. "And now, because this evening's lecture is a very special one, I am handing you over to my dear friend, Professor Suleiman."

Yusof stood up. He looked very slight alongside the burly Professor Profundo. He started to tell the students about his work, about the wonderful, magical even, healing properties of the plants in the forest. Like Professor Profundo, he spoke without notes, using slides on the computer, projected on to the big screen. Ibrahim was sure he had grown at least twice as tall as he had been, listening to his father. He was so proud to be his son. Yusof explained that his grandfather had been a bomoh in the kampong where they now lived. He explained that a bomoh was a kind of medicine man, a spiritual leader who could contact the spirit world, and who knew all the curative powers of all the plants in the forest. He explained that it was from his grandfather that he had learned so much about the healing properties of plants, especially forest plants. It was from him that he had been given the gift of passion about plants. He smiled fondly, remembering his wizened, toothless old grandfather. He explained that he was working, even now, on a cure for malaria, and for dengue fever, using plants from the forest.

"But now," he said, "we have problems never conceived of by my grandfather. As you are aware, the Asian forests are the most ancient in the world. They give us an incredibly rich eco system. Forests are being fired at a terrifying rate. At least 80,000 acres of forest are destroyed each day on a world wide basis. Make no mistake – that is 80,000 acres per day for three hundred and sixty five days of the year. Rain forests have more biodiversity than any other ecosystem. They are key to protecting the planet. Here in Malagiar, four fifths of the forest has already been replaced by palm oil plantations.

There is no doubt that palm oil brings wealth to the country. But we must not attain that wealth at the expense of the rain forest. We are destroying the balance of nature here. The rain forest provides us with substances which kill viruses, block cancer, combat neurological disease, depression, strokes, even lower blood pressure, and there are cures for many more ills. Did you know that, in South America, quinine was derived from the Cinchona tree – found deep in the Amazonian jungle? It is bad enough that we are firing the forests, but by doing so we are also creating more global warming, which, in turn, decreases dramatically the growth rate of many species."

He turned to the Professor, and nodded. The Professor jumped up, and stood beside Yusof.

"This is where the children come into the scheme of things" he said. Turning, he said "Joseph, will you tell the good people here your story?"

Joseph blushed furiously. He stood up and, turning, beckoned the others to stand alongside him. The Professor introduced the children to the audience, and then sat down alongside Yusof, leaving them to it.

"We know that the evil palm oil baron is trying to fire more of the forest" Joseph started. "He wants to fire five hundred thousand hectares".

There was a gasp from the audience.

"That means that he will just about wipe out the whole forest here in Malagiar. There are plants in there which are very valuable. There are animals. There are the Orang Asli, our friends."

Another gasp from the audience! Some of them had heard of the Orang Asli, but had never seen them.

"Apart from the destruction, can you imagine what it is like to be driven out of your home, to have your home burned down, even to be burned alive yourself? Some of the creatures of the forest are very slow. They cannot move quickly. When a fire starts, they get trapped. It is terrible, terrible! Professor Yusof is the head man of his kampong. The evil palm oil baron wants to burn down his kampong, which is on the edge of the forest, as well. We have already prevented the evil palm oil baron from starting his fires once, and we have, with the help of many, many people, dug a fire break through the forest, but the evil palm oil baron is intent on destroying everything in his path."

He turned to Ibrahim. Ibrahim chipped in

"Joseph is right. In my kampong, we look after the hurt and burned creatures of the forest. I help my father. I help him collect healing plants and herbs from the forest. We only use forest plants, and they really do heal. We rescued many animals from a fire, and they are nearly all healed. We have released those who can survive back into the forest, but some will never be able to fend for themselves again. We look after them. The evil palm oil baron wants to destroy all that."

Vinod could not contain himself.

"Yes, and I fell into an old bear pit, and Xin Hui rescued me, but then she got stuck in the pit, and Hitam Malam pulled her out."

Joseph and Ibrahim were dismayed. They had pledged that no mention would be made of the animals. But fortunately, nobody else seemed to notice the strange name, or ask who Hitam Malam was. A ripple of laughter ran through the audience. They had visions of Vinod, who was not particularly big, and Xin Hui, who was even smaller, scrabbling about at the bottom of a bear pit. Vinod, overwhelmed, turned back to his chair where he sat down quickly, with a bump. He did not know what had come over him.

Joseph continued. "We know that the evil palm oil baron and his men are going to fire the forest next week. They will be strong. They will bring fire throwing equipment and lots of other things, even guns I think. We are going to stop them." There was a cheer from the audience. "But we cannot do this on our own. We are asking all of you here to help us. It may be dangerous. You may get hurt. We already have lots of people who will help us, but we need more. If you would like to join us, gather at the kampong at five o'clock in the morning in a week's time."

There was a unanimous groan from the audience. Five o'clock! That was the middle of the night! Joseph sat down promptly. The others rushed to join him. Professor Profundo stood up, and drew the lecture to a close.

"Preservation of life, of all life, is essential to survival" he said, and reminded the students of the plan to meet at the kampong and ward off the evil palm oil baron. He was careful not to say "fight".

The Chancellor rose, resplendent in his robes, and started clapping. The students gave Professor Profundo, Professor Suleiman, and the children a standing ovation. The children squirmed. Professor Profundo laughed and waved, and Professor Suleiman bowed. The Chancellor told the students that details of the meeting to ward off the evil palm oil baron and his men would be posted on the notice board. Then he invited the two Professors and the children for a glass of sherry after the lecture. Professor Profundo accepted a large schooner of sherry, but Professor Suleiman took orange juice, as did the children.

Faradilla said "But when I grow up, I am going to be a veterinarian, not a botanist. I think Ibrahim might be a botanist, though." "My child" said the Chancellor. "That is wonderful. You will make an admirable veterinarian." He smiled fondly at that tiny scrap of a girl with so much spirit and determination, all dressed up in fuchsia with frangipani in her hair. She looked quite adorable. "And what about you other children? What are you all going to be?"

Joseph spoke first "I shall be a lawyer when I grow up." And Toby said, "I am going to be a botanist like my Dad". Ibrahim was not sure whether he would become a botanist or a doctor. Vinod definitely wanted to be a doctor, and Xin Hui was torn between being a doctor and a lawyer, "But I just might marry a rich man, lah, and never work," she said. They all laughed.

⚬⚬⚬⚬⚬⚬⚬⚬⚬⚬⚬⚬

Everyone agreed the Professor's lecture to the students had been a singular success. They were sitting around, discussing what they would do to prevent the evil palm oil baron next time, when Aishah came running down the path, waving a newspaper.

"Your friend, Shirley Pooper, has certainly been working hard." she called breathlessly. She laid the South East Asia Gazette down on a table. There were the headlines on the front page **"Doughty Warriors Fight Off Evil Palm Oil Baron and His Men."** The whole front page had been given to the battle with the evil palm oil baron's men, even the second and third page. There were photographs too, lots of them: photographs of Ibrahim and Tunku (Tunku's arm was wrapped round Ibrahim's shoulders), of Shirley Pooper herself, with Xin Hui and Faradilla perched on Cahaya Bulan's back, racing through the fire. There were photographs of Toby and Vinod firing catapults at the evil palm oil baron's men, and of Joseph and Ibrahim stamping out the fire as best they could. There was a photograph of some of the Orang Asli using blow pipes, and one of some macaques chucking down ripe mangos. Then, finally, the piece de resistance was a photograph of the elephants round the pit with the evil palm oil baron's men squatting down in it, followed by a photograph of the men running up the road as fast as they could, chased by the elephants. The children giggled to see the photographs. Bert was a very good photographer.

"Look at Tunku's face", giggled Xin Hui.

"Look at Matahari. My goodness, he looks angry with his ears out and his tail up."

"Is this her scoop, then?" asked Vinod. "She kept saying she wanted a scoop."

They laughed.

Shirley had described the whole battle.

Shirley had rounded off the article by writing

'This is modern day David and Goliath. These Doughty Warriors, Joseph, Ibrahim, Vinod, Xin Hui, Faradilla, and Toby, fighting the evil palm oil baron and his men are merely children; courageous, dedicated children, whom it has been my privilege to meet. Long may they continue their battle against this evil. And there is not a man or woman among us here in Malagiar who should not also be privileged to help them, or to know them. Their fight must continue, for the greater good.'

"My goodness," said Aishah. Yusof shook his head in amazement. The children were very excited. They had never had their names in newspapers before, let alone their photographs.

"Children, you realize this is serious." Yusof said. He explained to them that the publicity meant they would be known wherever they went, that they would now be hounded by hordes of journalists, that their names were exposed to the evil palm oil baron, that the involvement of the forest creatures had been exposed. Good things will come of this article, and bad things too. We have to be prepared."

Joseph was very glad that Yusof had said "We" rather than "You". It meant he was with them in this. Yusof told them all to telephone their parents immediately and explain about the article. It would be a big surprise to them! The Press would soon find out who they were and they, too, could well be hounded. Professor Profundo merely chuckled.

CHAPTER 16

In the offices of the South East Asia Gazette, Sam, the editor, was cock-a-hoop. He had already treated himself to a big, fat cigar. Puffing away happily, he slapped Shirley Pooper on the back, so hard that she fell forward. Bert caught her, just in time.

"You've done it this time, Kiddo." he said. "You've pulled it off. At last, you've got a really big scoop. And Bert, your photos are great, just great!" He beamed at them. "The morning edition has already sold out. Even now, we are running another print run. We are going to re-run this afternoon too, five times the normal quantity. I guarantee every newspaper will sell. There's nothing like children and animals to fuel the imagination. Wonderful! Wonderful!" He paused. "Here, I've bought Champagne to celebrate." He opened a bottle, the cork popped out with a big bang, and the golden, bubbly liquid fizzed over. They drank the champagne out of paper cups. Shirley was very pleased. Sam had never paid her so much attention before. Bert was very happy, too. He knew his photos were good, and that, because of the novelty value, they would be in demand, and he had many more as well. He would be able to sell some of them freelance. That would make him some money! Shirley was also thinking about money. *'I hope the old goat gives me a pay rise now. I need it. I think I shall go back to the kampong tomorrow. There is bound to be more happening there.'*

◦◦◦◦◦◦◦◦◦◦◦◦◦

Mr and Mrs Brown, Mr and Mrs Singh and Mr and Mrs Chan had arrived at the kampong. The children were very anxious. They had a lot of explaining to do. The Browns, the Singhs and the Chans had already seen the newspaper article. They had read it over breakfast. Mrs Brown had choked on her coffee when she read it, Mr Chan had knocked his over, and Mrs Chan had dropped the toast. Mrs Singh said she had not been able to eat breakfast at all, she felt so sick.

Yusof and Aishah, as ever, stepped into the fray. They said the children would never come to any harm as long as the Orang Asli and the creatures of the forest were with them. Indeed, the creatures had played a great part in protecting the children.

"Look at how Cahaya Bulan carried Xin Hui and Faradilla safely through the fires. And I know that you, Mrs Chan, are already fully confident in Cahaya Bulan".

Mrs Chan was very misty-eyed.

"The Orang Asli will never let them come to any harm. And Tunku and the elephant tribe will always keep watch over them. The forest is all-seeing. Aishah and I are fully confident that nothing bad will befall the children when they are in the forest."

The parents had to agree with Yusof. Mrs Singh gave Vinod a very big, very tight hug. He told her all about falling into the old bear pit. She went pale. Mr Singh looked very serious, but also gave his son a big hug. Mr and Mrs Chan clung to Xin Hui, their precious only daughter. They wished she had not got involved in all this but realised that, now that she had, there was no stopping her. Mrs Brown hugged Joseph, and Mr Brown stoically shook his hand. Yusof and Aishah stood with their hands on the shoulders of Faradilla and Ibrahim respectively, and Professor Profundo stood proudly with his hand on Toby's shoulder. He had a tear in his eye.

Yusof asked the parents if they had time to stay. They said they had. He had called a village meeting, he said. It would be necessary that everyone knew what to say, because reporters would surely be crawling all over the place very soon. They sat down in the padang and waited for the villagers to arrive. The parents sat very close to their children.

In the trees above, the monkeys, the birds, and the insects fell silent. They, too, were waiting. Then Tunku arrived, gliding silently as ever, through the trees. The head man from the Orang Asli was suddenly there, on the padang. The villagers arrived. They were all there. Yusof stepped forward.

"I want to thank you all for coming today, at such short notice. However, the occasion does warrant it. I presume you have all seen today's version of the South East Asia Gazette. I have no doubt at all that more journalists will very soon be arriving, asking questions, wanting more information. They will try to find their way into the forest, to find the Orang Asli and the creatures. We must be on our guard. We cannot allow them into the forest. They must know as little as possible about the special relationship these children have with the animals, and about the Orang Asli who want to be left in peace, to live as they have lived for thousands of years. If the journalists know nothing at all, that will be good. I think, however, it will be impossible.

I suggest we can tell them about the evil palm oil baron and his plans to fire five hundred thousand hectares of forest. After all, Shirley Pooper, has already mentioned that in her article. We can tell them about the bravery and dedication of the children in fighting off the evil palm oil baron. We can tell them about the involvement of the villagers, the city folk, and everyone else who has helped us. We can tell them that we have dug a fire break to prevent the fires from spreading. But it is best not to tell them where the fire break is. I also propose to tell them that we are starting a charity to look after those creatures too badly hurt to fend for themselves, and to carry on the essential work of botanical exploration which Professor Profundo and I are conducting. We must not tell them anything at all about the Orang Asli and the creatures. Is everyone agreed on this?"

Throughout the crowd, there were murmurs of consent. Yusof's proposals were very sensible. Yusof looked up, and groaned.

"Oh no. I think I see some of them coming already. Quickly, everyone. Do not let them see that we have been having a meeting."

The crowd dispersed, the villagers went about their business. The parents gathered up their offspring and headed for home.

The children did not mind. They had not been home for a while, and they wanted to check their e.mails, and Vinod wanted to check out his new little brother. Professor Profundo, Yusof, Ibrahim and Toby headed off into the forest to gather plants. Aishah and Faradilla disappeared into the kitchen. Within less than ten minutes nobody would have known there had been a big meeting on the padang.

A couple of seedy reporters headed down the main street of the village. It was all very peaceful. Nothing was going on here. They asked questions, but the villagers said they did not understand. The reporters went away. Maybe they had come to the wrong kampong.

❧❧❧❧❧❧❧❧❧

At home, Joseph, Vinod and Xin Hui were checking their e.mails. They had hundreds and hundreds. Joseph started to plough through his. One or two were from cranks, telling him he was a 'nutter', and why did he not leave well alone. Palm oil is beneficial to modern life. But, by and large, the e.mails were encouraging. Congratulations and offers of help were the largest sector.

Vinod and Xin Hui found the same thing. Ibrahim had promised to check his e.mails when he returned from the forest.

'I will get together with the others this evening. Perhaps we can send out another e.mail.' Joseph thought. *'We shall need more help when the next battle comes, next week.'*

CHAPTER

The evil palm oil baron was in a very good mood. He rubbed his hands together gleefully. He was about to dine with the Prime Minister. He had arranged a private room at a very exclusive, very discreet restaurant, and had arrived early to check that everything was organised as planned.

The chandelier was twinkling, crystal shards throwing delicate light patterns around the walls. The gold silk curtains were drawn. Two beautiful arrangements of gold and white roses were set against the drawn curtains. The table was laid with a crisp white cloth, gold and white porcelain, silver cutlery, and finest crystal glasses. Crisp white table napkins were laid on each side plate in the form of a lotus flower, with a yellow rose lying beside it. The candles were lit – low candles, not tall ones. A low bowl of yellow and white roses was in the middle of the table. The palm oil baron wanted nothing to break the visual contact he would have with the Prime Minister. He had organised the menu in advance. He knew precisely what the Prime Minister liked, and made sure it was all there. They were to have an eight course meal. He was superstitious. Eight

was a lucky number, and eight courses would give him the time he needed to win the Prime Minister over to his latest project. Everything was perfect. The evil palm oil baron smiled happily to himself.

He had on one of his best Boss suits, a new shirt and a gold tie – to harmonise with the surroundings. He plucked a golden rose from the display on a side table and placed it in his button-hole. His hair was brushed back. The sticking plaster had gone. He had even had the maid polish his shoes.

The Prime Minister arrived. His minder inspected the room, then withdrew discreetly, closing the door behind him. Only the most trusted waiters would attend them. The dishes would all be checked in the kitchens prior to arrival in the dining room.

"My Dear Prime Minister. My Dear Teo!" the evil palm oil baron held out his hand.

"Lee, What can I do for you? For surely, (looking around) feting me as you are, there is something you want."

The evil palm oil baron giggled.

"Prime Minister. Clearly, you do not know me at all. This is a dinner of gratitude, for all that you have helped me with in the past, and, indeed, only recently you signed the approval for the next tract of palm oil to be planted."

"You mean I signed the approval for the next colossal tract of forest to be burned down." said the Prime Minister.

Lee giggled again. The conversation was not going as he had planned.

"Prime Minister! Prime Minister! You make it sound so terrible. But there is always plenty of forest. Let us drink to success, to lots of money." He held out an ice-encrusted glass filled with sparkling champagne to the Prime Minister. "Your health!" he raised his glass in a toast.

"And how did you enjoy your holiday on the yacht?" he asked, archly. "I hope everything was to your satisfaction."

The Prime Minister felt uncomfortable. How had he got into this mess, beholden to the palm oil baron? It was becoming political – dangerous. He was far too much in this man's debt. *'If it should ever come out!'* He shuddered.

"Yes, we enjoyed our sojourn on the yacht. My wife particularly enjoyed it. I am aware of how indebted to you we are. I would be most grateful if you would accept payment for that holiday. I will have my secretary send you a cheque tomorrow."

This was not quite what the evil palm oil baron wanted to hear. He had expected a little more grovelling gratitude from the Prime Minister.

"Prime Minister, I will not even consider it. I should be offended to take money from you."

"But I insist, Lee. I absolutely insist."

They sat down at the table. The first course was brought in. The evil palm oil baron took his time, massaging the Prime Minister's ego, telling him what a wonderful job he was doing, holding the nation together, fending off the opposition. He was quite sure that, at the next election, everyone would vote to retain their existing Prime Minister. He wanted the Prime Minister to be very mellow when he broached his next request. He had already instructed the waiter to keep the Prime Minister's glass topped up all the time. He raised another toast.

CHAPTER 17

"To your next term in office!" The Prime Minister drank only the smallest sip. The waiter topped up the Prime Minister's glass.

"Prime Minister, I have just purchased a magnificent villa, right on the top of a mountain, and surrounded by forest. The air there is as exquisite as this champagne. The evenings are so cool, they even have to light log fires to keep warm. It is quite exceptional. You should go and see it, stay there. I know your wife would love it, and it would be a change from the heat and humidity here in Malagiar."

The Prime Minister's discomfort grew. He was only too conscious of his talk with Professor Profundo. What was it the palm oil baron wanted? He would not be trying to bribe him already, unless he wanted something very badly. He decided to be careful. He asked the waiter for a bottle of water.

"Thank you, Lee. You are very kind. But my engagements are taking up all my time at present. I cannot see the likelihood of getting away for several months."

"Never mind, Prime Minister. In your own time! But I insist that you go there. You will love it." He changed the subject.

"Let me tell you about my newest project. It is very daring."

The waiter continued, discreetly removing dishes, replacing them with new ones, pouring the champagne. The Prime Minister whispered something in his ear. The waiter nodded.

"And what is that?" asked the Prime Minister.

"You are familiar with Black Rock Island?"

The Prime Minister nodded. He recalled that Black Rock

Island was uninhabited, a forested land mass of about two hundred square miles. It was part of the National Park. The seas around it were teeming with wild life. Rumour had it that there were rich mineral deposits there.

"I am buying it. I need your permission to drill for oil. Not that there is any, but it might be worth a try."

'So that's it. That is what he is after'.

"What makes you think oil is there? Drilling is an expensive business. You would not drill unless you were very sure."

The evil palm oil baron considered the extensive research he had done, the vast sums of money he had already paid his researchers, to find oil on the island, but he was not about to tell the Prime Minister. He shrugged his shoulders.

"Prime Minister. I am an entrepreneur. I take risks, calculated risks, but risks nonetheless."

"Am I correct in understanding that Black Rock Island is part of the National Park? How are you managing to buy it?"

This conversation was definitely not going the way the evil palm oil baron wanted it. He changed position in his chair.

"Oh, you know, Prime Minister, there are ways and means."

"Ah! Who did you bribe this time?"

The verbal assault by the Prime Minister was direct and unexpected. He had never behaved like this previously. The evil palm oil baron was uncomfortable. The waiter came in, bearing a newspaper. He handed it to the Prime Minister.

"Thank you, Andrew" said the Prime Minister. "Tell me, Lee, have you seen today's papers?"

"No, Prime Minister. I cannot say that I have. I have been very busy today."

"No doubt tying up your Black Rock Island deal."

The evil palm oil baron giggled weakly "Oh, Prime Minister, you have such a sense of humour."

"Nevertheless, you should see today's paper." He held it up for the evil palm oil baron to see. The headlines were clear and easy to read **"Doughty Warriors Fight Off Evil Palm Oil Baron and His Men"**.

The evil palm oil baron blanched. He pulled at his tie again. He stroked back his hair. Snatching the paper from the Prime Minister, he read the whole article before he let out a howl of rage. He threw the newspaper down.

"What nonsense! I shall sue! This is defamation of character! Prime Minister, you cannot possibly believe this rubbish. It is patent lies, all of it."

The Prime Minister remained calm. "Mud sticks, Lee." he said. "Now, if you do not mind, I have another pressing engagement. Thank you for dinner."

He called his aide, who was immediately at his side, to show him out.

The evil palm oil baron was left on his own in the private dining room of the exclusive restaurant. They had only eaten two of the eight courses he had organised. He was in such a rage that he swept all the crockery, the porcelain, the crystal glasses, the rose bowl and the candles off the table in one sweep of his arm. It came crashing down to the floor. He stormed out of the room, leaving the mess in his wake.

The following day, the evil palm oil baron received a very, very large bill from the restaurant for the meal, and for all the damage he had done.

He was fuming with rage. E.mails from all sorts of unknown individuals were still flooding into his offices, disrupting business, clogging the computers. Newspaper reporters were constantly on the telephone demanding interviews. Business colleagues were telephoning him, demanding to know if the newspaper allegations were true.

"Get me Ah Kong" he screamed at his manager. The poor man ran from the evil palm oil baron's office grateful that the telephone directory the evil palm oil baron had thrown at him had missed. Ah Kong arrived.

"What is the meaning of this?" he screamed at Ah Kong, stubbing at the article with his pudgy fore finger.

"We were caught unawares, Sir. But we have everything under control. We did not know they would be there, or that they would use elephants. We are going back next week with flame throwers, and with guns. We shall be taking three hundred men. I think that will be enough to get rid of those pestilent children." Ah Kong was shaking in his boots.

"Get rid of them. Do what you like. But get rid of them. Do you hear me? Get rid of them." He threw the big glass ashtray at Ah Kong. Ah Kong ducked. The ash tray hit a picture on the wall, and broke the glass. The evil palm oil baron screamed. Ah Kong fled. The last words he heard the evil palm oil baron screaming were

"Five hundred   thousand hectares. Do you hear? Five hundred thousand, and nothing less."

CHAPTER 18

"Ayah is talking to the head man of the Orang Asli today. But we need to get all the villagers, and the people from the city, and the people from the Mosque to help" said Ibrahim.

"And from the Temple" added Xin Hui.

"I'll speak to the priest again" offered Joseph

"And I shall speak to the priest at the Hindu temple, and the Granthi at the Gurdwara," Vinod said.

"We can do that now" said Joseph. "Let's go. We'll meet up again at twelve o'clock, for lunch, at the kampong."

The children assembled again at lunchtime. Aishah, as always, had prepared lunch for them. They were pleased with themselves. Everyone they had spoken to had read yesterday's newspaper. Everyone had congratulated them, and was prepared to help. It was a nice feeling to be popular, in the public eye.

"They are going to come with guns and flame-throwers this time, but my Dad says we must not use weapons. We can only use tools like our catapults, and spades and sticks and stones. We will have to form a line in front of the fire break, here I have been thinking about this. Do you think, Ibrahim, that the Orang Asli would dig some bear pits in front of our line?"

Joseph drew lines in the dust with a stick, first the fire break, then the line where they would all be posted, and in front of that line, he drew a line of small circles.

"Those are the bear pits, camouflaged, of course. And what about the creatures? Will they help us again?"

Wholly absorbed, the children did not see the seedy reporter and his photographer making their way stealthily down the street. The photographer's camera was poised, focused on the children. He raised it to his eye. At that moment, there was a shout.

"Oi! You! Get out of here." The children looked up to see the reporter and his cameraman running back up the street, with Shirley Pooper, frizzy dyed blonde hair jigging up and down, in hot pursuit, brandishing her handbag, swinging it about her head. They laughed. Finally, when she had seen the competition off, she stopped, out of breath. Bending down, she placed her hands on her knees while she recovered. Straightening up, she turned towards the children and waved. She headed towards them.

"Hi, Kids! I'm getting pretty practiced at seeing people off. I promise you, no-one else will get even a foot in the door. This is MY scoop!"

She was positively grinning now, from ear to ear.

"Bert will be coming in a while, but I wanted to talk to you first. How do you feel after that last fight? Did you like my article? What are you doing next? How will you fight off the evil palm oil baron next time?"

Her notebook came out, pencil poised already.

"Whoa, whoa! Steady on!" said Joseph, laughing. "One question at a time."

Xin Hui giggled, hiding her face behind her hand. The others were all laughing openly. Shirley joined in the mirth.

"Ah well, just say I'm excited," she said. "That was a great scoop. My boss might even give me a pay rise."

She held out her hand, ruefully examining her broken finger nails. She showed them to the children.

"But there was a high price to pay!"

She sighed theatrically, tossing back her unruly hair. The children simply carried on laughing. It was good to laugh.

"If we tell you our plans, Shirley, you must promise not to publish until after the next fight is all over," said Joseph. "The evil palm oil baron must not get wind of what we are doing."

Shirley sat, hand on heart, looking suddenly very serious "Joseph, I promise. I give you my solemn promise."

That was good enough for Joseph. He looked at Ibrahim and Toby, who nodded their assent. Bert arrived. Once everyone had settled down, Joseph started to talk. In a large degree, he was outlining his plan as he went along. The others listened, nodded, interjected occasionally. They felt the plan was sound. Ibrahim volunteered to tell Tunku what was to happen, and he, in turn, would pass the message on to Matahari. Within only hours, the whole forest would be aware of the plan.

"And Ayah will tell the Orang Asli." he said. "I know they will help us.'

"You are quite the General, Joseph. Well done." Bert said.

"But we do not know when the evil palm oil baron's men will come, lah!" said Xin Hui.

"That is a problem. I know it will be next week – but when next week?" Joseph replied. He scratched his head.

"Ah, I think I may be able to help you," said Bert. "I know where Ah Kong and his men go drinking. Perhaps I shall drop in there, do a little bit of spying."

"But they will recognise you."

"Aha! I am a master of disguise. I shall have a bit of a stoop, and I shall sit in a corner, out of the light. With a little bit of make-up, my grey wig, an eye patch, and bushy eyebrows, I defy anybody to recognise me." Bert grinned. He was going to enjoy this.

"I'll come with you" Shirley said.

"No. I shall go alone. They will definitely recognise you."

"Oh, Boo!" she said.

The children laughed again. This was fun.

Yusof and Professor Profundo came strolling out of the forest, carrying lots of strange looking plants, very pleased with themselves. Joseph introduced the Professor to Shirley Pooper and Bert. Yusof suggested they should go with him and the Professor, down to the nursery, where he had planted young plants, in an effort to preserve as many species as possible, should the forest be burned down. He thought it might be a good idea for Shirley Pooper to write about that in her paper. Gratefully, she trotted along behind him. Another exclusive! Oh boy! She called Bert to come with her. He could take some photos of Yusof and Professor Profundo. After all, Professor Profundo was an eminent man!

Ah Kong was in the bar with his mate, a big, brawny man. They were both drinking whisky on ice. *'They've had quite a few already.'* Bert thought as he watched and waited. *'That should loosen their tongues.'* Sure enough, Ah Kong soon started talking about the big battle to come next week. He was determined to wipe out 'those demon children'. Bert listened attentively.

"What time do you want us there, Mate?" asked the big, brawny fellow.

"We will start early. Make it six o'clock sharp on Monday. I want to get this over and done with as quickly as possible." Ah Kong was looking grim.

AND, the palm oil baron has assured me that, should we need it, the army will back us up. They will be waiting on stand-by. I only have to make the call. We will wipe out those wretched children and their jungle pets in no time."

'The army! Oh dear! Oh dear! Do those children know what they are letting themselves in for? He corrected himself. *'What are WE letting ourselves in for?'* Bert swigged down his pint, and left discreetly without being noticed. He now had the time and date of the big fight. He had no doubt, from what he had heard in that bar, that it would be a very big fight indeed. He was worried. Journalists and the media should always remain impartial, but he was becoming very fond of those feisty children. *'What if one of them got shot? What if HE got shot? Or even Shirley Pooper? Oh dear! Oh dear!'*

CHAPTER 19

It was four-thirty in the morning, still dark. Dawn had not yet broken. The padang was full of people, gloomy shadows in a surreal half light cast by lanterns, as far as the eye could see. The villagers were there, city folk, people from the mosque, from the temples, from the church, students from the university. They were armed with all manner of things: some carried garden spades and forks, some carried stout staves, some carried ropes. Many women carried a saucepan or a frying pan, and a metal spoon or fork They were very quiet, thinking, no doubt, of what was to come. Those who had been present last time, knew roughly what to expect, but the others had no idea. The parents were there, and Yusof and Professor Profundo. Shirley Pooper and Bert were there somewhere, running around, taking photos.

Even a week ago, Joseph would have been terrified at the prospect of facing so many, let alone speaking to them. But now he was filled with a kind of quiet pride. He looked about him. Everyone was still, quiet. Yusof nodded to him. This time, Joseph had a loudspeaker to speak through.

CHAPTER 19

"Ladies and Gentlemen" he began. "Today we are going to take on the evil palm oil baron's men. They have promised a hard fight." He paused. "But they do not know how determined we are. They do not know that the Orang Asli and the creatures of the forest would rather die now, if they have to, than burn slowly and horribly to death in their own forest. For the forest does belong to them. You all know the plan and where you are posted. Do not worry when you see the creatures. They can look quite scary, but they will not hurt any of us. They are with us. And the Orang Asli. They look fierce, but they are people too, who just want to be left alone to live their lives as they always have done."

People like Mrs Chan and Mrs Brown, who had already experienced working alongside the animals, had their own special memories.

"You all know what to do. You have been allocated a team leader. Stick with your leader. Each team leader will have a team of animals and Orang Asli waiting for him in the forest. The Orang Asli will line up behind us. You probably will not even see them, but they will be there. And the animals will line up behind the Orang Asli. To start with, the evil Palm oil baron's men will not see any of us from the road. They will think they are alone. Team leaders, please come to the front, and, as you collect your people together, head off into the forest, along the pathway at the bottom of the kampong. Good luck, everyone!" Joseph ended his speech. Now he started to shake. It was nerves, he knew, but still he was shaking.

The team leaders gathered at the front of the padang. Mr Brown and Mr Chan were there, as were Mr Singh, Yusof, and Professor Profundo. As previously, ten people from the village and from the city were in each team, backed up by ten Orang Asli. Two elephants were also allocated to each team, but the other animals would fight simply where they felt it would be best.

Over the past few days, Joseph, Ibrahim and Yusof had worked everything out very carefully with the head man of the Orang Asli, and Tunku and Matahari had been very busy indeed. There was nothing left to do now, but head off into the forest. Dawn was gently banishing the night, and the forest was strangely quiet. It was shady and cool in the forest, but very dry. There had been no rain for weeks. Yusof and the Orang Asli were worried. The forest being so dry meant that fires would spread more easily.

Moreover, Bert had told them what he had overheard in the bar. The evil palm oil baron would go to any lengths to get his way. The army would undoubtedly be brought in. Would they really shoot children, women, the creatures? What was the world coming to? The head man of the Orang Asli told Yusof that the more he saw of the modern world, the less he liked it. Yusof had to agree. It was all mad, bizarre.

Within a very short time, everyone was in position and settled down to wait. Those who could, squatted on their haunches. Professor Profundo chuckled when Yusof squatted down.

"All my life, I have wanted to do that, and I have never been able to get the balance right. I topple over every time."

The children kept a keen look-out for the Orang Asli and the animals, but they could see nothing. Nonetheless, they knew they were there. Joseph could feel their presence; he was quite sure there were bristles standing straight up on the back of his neck. They were standing or sitting in lines, the humans about twenty yards back from the road-side, the Orang Asli were another twenty yards behind them, and the animals ten yards behind the Orang Asli, immediately in front of the fire break. The plan was that, if all else failed, they would retreat behind the fire-break, and continue fighting from there. He had wanted to leave Faradilla and Xin Hui in the village, but they would have none of it. They were there, too, perched in the branches of a tree. Vinod was standing, waiting, with clenched fists, and Toby looked a little pale. Ibrahim was calm and collected.

"Does it hurt when you get shot?" Vinod whispered.

"I think so, but none of us will get shot, so do not worry" Ibrahim whispered back.

They heard the sound of the lorries before they saw them. Everyone tensed, and stood up, craning their necks to see. There were a lot of men climbing out of the lorries. They were dragging equipment out.

"Not yet; not yet" whispered Joseph. They waited.

"Now!" shouted Joseph. At once the women who had them, started banging on their saucepans and frying pans as hard and as loud as they could. At the same time, they shouted with all their might. The Siamang boomed in the trees. The noise was deafening. The elephants, whom nobody could see, set up a magnificent trumpeting. The very foundations of the forest rocked with all the noise. Bears growled, tigers snarled, the monkeys and birds in the trees set up a piercing racket. Faradilla put her hands over her ears.

The evil palm oil baron's men, startled, stepped back. Some leapt straight back into the lorries. But Ah Kong roared at them. They got out again. They did not look very confident. Ah Kong roared orders at the top of his voice. He was not going to put up with this. He was not going to allow silly children to outwit him. By sheer strength of will, he mobilised his men. They lined up, clubs and flame-throwers in hand. The children let loose their catapults. Small stones found their mark, annoying the men, but still they continued, lighting the flame-throwers. Overhead, Tunku, Number One Son, and their cousins had collected stock piles of coconuts and pineapples. They were throwing them now with all their might. Many found their mark, several of the evil palm oil baron's men were knocked out. The monkeys were throwing anything they could get their little hands on: guavas, mangosteen, mangoes, nuts, stones, sticks. The trees appeared to be raining fruit, nuts, sticks and stones relentlessly. But it was not enough. There were so many men.

The children and their army advanced. More of the evil palm oil baron's men were arriving. They carried rifles. The army arrived. They, too, carried guns. Joseph watched as columns of great forest ants marched relentlessly forward, protecting their territory from these evil men. Anything that got in their way was bitten. Several of the evil palm oil baron's men jumped up and down, wailing in anguish as the ants got to them. Ah Kong, grabbing a soldier's rifle from him, shot it into the air, hoping to frighten the children.

Before any of the soldiers could take aim, the Buddhist monks rushed out of the forest, and tackled them. With swift karate chops, leg kicks, and all manner of exciting moves, they disarmed the men, knocking their guns out of their hands. The Sikhs were behind them, the warrior race, fighting hand to hand as they went. Muslims, too, wiry, hardened men, were fighting, defending the forest. Joseph saw the Catholic priest locked in arm to arm combat with one of the evil palm oil baron's men. The villagers came on, and the city folk. It was hand to hand fighting now. Mrs Chan was swiping with a frying pan at anybody who got in her way. Mrs Brown stood, feet planted firmly, alongside her, swinging another frying pan with all her might. Mrs Singh stood alongside her husband, Mr Singh. How she would fight! She would die for him, for her son, and even for the forest if necessary. Mr Brown and Mr Chan fought with a grim determination. Yusof and Professor Profundo only had to think of the destruction a fire would cause to become incensed. They fought hard. Professor Profundo was not in the best condition. He puffed a lot.

Some of the evil palm oil baron's men had regained their rifles. Panicked, they started to fire wildly, not aiming at anything specific.

From the trees, an army of fruit bats flew down, their wide wingspan obliterating all sight, uncharacteristically biting and snapping with their teeth. The men again dropped their guns, arms flailing. The Orang Asli had come up. Their blow pipes were not deadly, but the darts were very uncomfortable. They were fighting hand to hand as well. Small and wiry, they were like slithery eels to the evil palm oil baron's men. More of them arrived. Grasping their rifles, they tumbled from the lorries.

The creatures of the forest could stand no more. They emerged angrily from the dense undergrowth. The noise was still deafening. Monkeys overhead were throwing everything they could lay their hands on, screeching as they did so. Tunku had called up his cousins. Between them, they were bombarding the evil palm oil baron's men with sticks and foliage, coconuts, pineapples, mangoes, nuts, and anything else they could lay their hands on. Tunku had never worked so hard in his life. He hurled lethal missile after lethal missile. The bears and tigers charged, snarling. The elephants charged, trunks raised, ears flapping, trumpeting loudly. Porcupines rattled around the ground, thrusting their sharp spines into the evil palm oil baron's mens' legs.

Shirley Pooper and Bert were running up and down the lines. She was shouting into a mouthpiece "And now the soldiers are here! Oh My God! It cannot be possible! How can soldiers fight children and women? How can they fight animals? I do not believe this. What is the world coming to? What is the government of Malagiar thinking of, turning the army on its own people?" She was shrieking. The noise around her was deafening.

Several sections of the forest were blazing. The flame throwers were deadly.

"We have got to put the flame throwers out of action." screamed Joseph – to anyone who might hear him. Matahari heard. Ibrahim was already on his back. Rushing up to

Joseph, Matahari scooped him up. Ribut, Halilintar, and Rijaksana joined him. Vinod was mounted on Ribut, Toby on Halilintar, and Professor Profundo on Rijaksana.

'Oh my goodness, what a jolly time this is! If only my University friends could see me now!' thought the Professor.

The four elephants charged the flame-throwers. Bears and tigers tackled soldiers. Then the forest rhinos stampeded out of the forest, gathering speed as they came. They charged! The soldiers fired wildly before turning to flee, along with the evil palm oil baron's men. Many of them fell. But they were able to regroup again and again. By now the soldiers were entirely mixed up with the evil palm oil baron's men.

The forest was blazing. The children, the villagers and city folk, the Orang Asli and the creatures were fighting for their very lives. But they would not give up. On and on they fought.

"Oh no!" cried Xin Hui. The bole of the tree in which she and Faradilla were perched, had caught fire. The girls prepared to jump. It was a long way down. Then, there beneath them, just in time, was Cahaya Bulan. They jumped on to her back, and she carried them to a safer place, gently depositing them behind a big tree. Several of the villagers and animals were wounded or shot. The Orang-Asli fought fiercely, giving no quarter. Many of the evil palm oil baron's men and the soldiers lay wounded or unconscious on the ground.

"Retreat! Retreat!" shouted Joseph. Their whole itinerant army retreated back to behind the fire-break, the evil palm oil baron's men and the soldiers in hot pursuit. Faradilla and Xin Hui were waiting for them. They had tied a strong liana around the boles of two trees, about thirty feet apart. Mrs Brown and Mrs Chan were with them, the liana was about twelve inches above the ground. As the evil palm oil baron's men and the soldiers ran on, Faradilla and Xin Hui pulled hard. The men tripped over the tightly stretched liana and fell to the ground. Mrs Brown and

CHAPTER 19

Mrs Chan hopped out from their hiding place behind the tree and whacked them over the head with their frying pans. The men were all knocked out. They did this again and again. They knocked out a lot of men. Then Aishah and Mrs Singh joined them. The women all clutched frying pans, determined, ready to fight to the death. They were panting, pink-cheeked, but adrenalin was flowing; they would never back down. Never!

Ah Kong was delighted. He saw the children's army fleeing, as he thought. Whooping with glee, he and his men raced after them. The animals were waiting. They charged forward again, in front of the humans, snarling, snapping, tearing with claws, they fought to the death to defend their forest. A civet cat crumpled at Mrs Brown's feet. It had been shot. A huge bear was limping badly, but still fighting. Ribut had a nasty slash across his flank. Matahari was hit by a bullet, and then another. He screamed in pain and rage. Joseph and Ibrahim, sitting astride him, were shaken. But Matahari fought on. Above the deafening noise of the battle, Joseph heard a loud hum, a sort of droning noise.

'It's the bees! It's the bees!" shouted Ibrahim, delighted!

An enormous, dense, black cloud flew over them, darkening the sky as it went. The bees flew on, only descending when they reached the evil palm oil baron's men and the soldiers. The children could hear wails and screams of torment and terror as the bees attacked, stinging their prey, driving them mad with pain and with fear. Every bee was prepared to sacrifice its life to save the forest. Every bee which stung, died almost immediately. They could only ever sting once. But still they carried on stinging.

'Such brave little bees' thought Ibrahim.

A cortege of black cars drew up on the road. A large black limousine with the Malagiar flag on the front was in the middle of the cortege. The fighting in the forest continued unabated. A slightly built man in a dark grey suit, with thinning hair and spectacles stepped out of the big black limousine. Surrounded by bodyguards, he stood for a few minutes, looking about him, watching. He could see the fires raging; he could see people fighting each other; he could see soldiers fighting locals; he could see some of the Orang Asli and some of the creatures. He gasped as Matahari and Ribut emerged, with three small boys on top, chasing soldiers back to the roadside. He said something to an unobtrusive man who had moved up alongside him. Within seconds, men moved away from the cars. They spoke to the soldiers, and their commanders. The soldiers withdrew.

They found Ah Kong and spoke to him – a few choice words! Ah Kong rallied his men, and they withdrew. Climbing into the lorries, the soldiers and the evil palm oil baron's men made off. They left their flame throwers and equipment, even some rifles, behind.

Yusof and Professor Profundo, both now astride Rijaksana, in hot pursuit of Ah Kong, emerged from the forest. They raced through flames, Rijaksana trumpeting angrily, the Professor brandishing a large club, Yusof, in front of him, urging Rijaksana on. Yusof pulled Rijaksana up when he saw the cortege of cars and the slightly built man in the grey suit.

"Why, Prime Minister, what are you doing here?" called Professor Profundo.

Yusof said something to Rijaksana, who lowered Yusof and the Professor to the ground. Rijaksana did not go away. He stayed, and waited for Yusof and the Professor. He had promised Matahari that he would look after them.

CHAPTER 19

"Professor Profundo, Yusof!" the Prime Minister said, "Would you do me the honour of dining with me tomorrow evening, at the Residence, say, at eight o'clock?"

Yusof and the Professor were taken aback. They looked at each other. Yusof answered for both of them

"Yes, Prime Minister. Thank you. We shall be there. But, forgive me for saying this, I think you should ask the children also. It is the children you need to speak to. It is the children who are our future."

"Very well" said the Prime Minister. "How many children are there?"

"There are six of them, Prime Minister."

"I shall see you all at eight, or, perhaps, as there are children, shall we make it seven-thirty?" The Prime Minister turned and climbed back into his limousine.

"Seven-thirty it is." said Yusof.

Nobody could believe that the evil palm oil baron's men and the soldiers had withdrawn so suddenly. They were suspicious, thinking it was a ruse, a trap. But Yusof and the Professor, astride Rijaksana again, told them that the Prime Minister had ordered the retreat. Nobody could quite believe what they heard. Joseph started to cheer, the other children, and then everyone else joined in, the animals too. The noise this time was definitely happy and triumphant, not the terrible menacing noise they had made before.

"But we have got to put the fires out before we do anything else" said Ibrahim. He felt something on his nose. A big plop! He looked up, black clouds were gathering overhead, and this time it was not the bees.

"Rain! It is starting to rain" he cried, delightedly.

"Rain! Rain!" the people picked up the chorus. Tunku and his cousins did a kind of rain dance in the trees. The monkeys joined in. The birds, stretching out their wings to catch the first great plops of rain, ruffling their feathers, danced up and down on the branches.

The bears stood on their hind legs, reaching up to the sky. Even the cats stretched themselves out as if to catch every drop of rain that came their way. Elephants trumpeted and flapped their ears, rhinos snorted and tossed their heads, pawing the ground. The Orang Asli did a sort of stamping dance, whooping gleefully at the same time. And all the other people cheered. They cheered and cheered. Faradilla thought they would never stop.

The fire break started to fill up with water, first a tiny little trickle, then getting bigger and stronger.

"If this rain keeps up, it will be full by tomorrow." Ibrahim said.

Collecting up their tools, the discarded flame-throwers and rifles, the frying pans and saucepans, the people slowly headed off, back to the kampong. Reluctant to leave the creatures of the forest behind, they were all amazed at what they had seen, in awe of the magnificence of what they had been a part of.

The creatures melted quietly into the forest, but not before Ibrahim had spoken to Tunku and to Matahari. He promised them that, the next day, he and Yusof would come to the glade with medicines and salves for the wounded creatures. Matahari was limping badly, the shot in his shoulder was hurting. But he could wait until the morning.

Then Joseph remembered the evil palm oil baron's men and the soldiers still in the bear pits. Nobody had let them out. He called out to Yusof, who, in turn spoke to the head of the Orang Asli. The men chuckled. The head man summoned his people, and they took off at a trot for the bear pits. The men at the bottom were in a sorry state, wet now from the rain, and jibbering and jabbering with fear. Snakes still clinging to the sides of the pits prohibited any attempt at escape. When they saw the Orang Asli coming, the snakes slithered off into the jungle. The Orang Asli lowered liana ladders down into the pits for the men to climb out. At first, they were too frightened to make a move, but then they scrambled up the ladders, pushing and shoving each other in their haste to escape, tumbling out of the pits with no dignity at all. The Orang Asli stood in a line, backs to the forest, spears, bows and arrows, and blow pipes at the ready. The terrified men turned and ran, making for the road. There was no need to chase them. They were running as fast as they possibly could.

Whilst the others were fighting, some of the village women had remained behind at the kampong. When everyone returned, they found great vats of water to wash in, and then, set around the padang, tables laden with simple fare, and plenty of fresh water to drink. Everybody was hungry, exultant, desperately needing to talk, to talk with wonder of what they had seen and done, what they had been a part of.

All of them were talking together, Buddhist, Moslem, Christian, Sikh, students, village folk and city folk, even the Orang Asli joined in. They had won the battle to prevent the evil palm oil baron from burning down the forest! What a celebration they had! It went on well into the night.

The children were exhausted. Joseph made a little speech, saying 'thank –you' to everyone for their help. Ibrahim, Vinod, Xin Hui, Faradilla, and Toby stood beside him. When he had finished, everyone in the padang stood up and clapped and cheered. Joseph blushed. The other children looked at the ground and shuffled their feet.

The parents took them off to bed because, as Yusof said

"There is a lot of work to be done tomorrow. We have many wounded animals to treat, and I shall need your help."

Joseph and the Orang Asli

CHAPTER 20

Shirley Pooper and Bert were exhausted, but still they worked through the night. They had to catch the morning's papers. They had so much to tell. Another scoop! Sam would be pleased.Shirley, still in a state of shock that women, children, and animals had been set upon by the soldiers, was determined to tell the story as it was. She typed long into the night. Bert, in his dark room, turned out photograph after photograph.

The morning edition of the South East Asia Gazette had a special edition insert, eight full pages devoted to the fight to preserve the forest from the evil palm oil baron, the involvement of the soldiers, of the Orang Asli and of the creatures of the forest, as well as the children, the villagers, and even city folk. Shirley left no stone unturned. Bert's photographs were spectacular. He had taken photographs of the evil palm oil baron's men throwing flames at the forest and at the creatures. He had taken photographs of the animals retaliating, and of the people fighting: the monks, the sikhs, the moslems, the catholic priest, the Orang Asli, of Yusof fighting with a great stave, of Professor Profundo charging on top of Rijaksana. And, of course, he had taken photographs of the children and of the elephants. He had a photo of Faradilla and Xin Hui pulling hard on the end of the liana to trip the evil palm oil baron's men. He had photographs of Vinod, riding Ribut, brandishing a stick. He had photographs of Ibrahim, Joseph, and Toby on Matahari and Halilintar. He had photographs of the women brandishing their frying pans. And, of course, he had photographs of the Prime Minister turning Ah Kong and his men away.

The story was dramatic. The photographs were magnificent. Sam was ecstatic. Shirley Pooper was certainly the best reporter he had ever employed, and Bert the best photographer. *'What a team!'*

"You are both definitely getting handsome pay rises." He shouted across the cutting floor. "We are going to print ten times as many papers as usual today. I guarantee every one will sell. Whooppee!!" he whooped. "I'm taking you guys out to dinner tonight. We are going to celebrate!"

All that Shirley and Bert could think of was getting to bed and getting some sleep. Their job was done; they had the scoop! Another one. They knew that once the story was published, every reporter, and probably television camera crew, within miles, would be checking the story. They would no longer have exclusive rights. But they had got the best part. They told Sam they were going home, to sleep.

"Of course. Of course" he cried "Off you go. We'll meet for dinner at seven thirty."

Copies of the South East Asia Gazette were flying off the

news stands. Who were these children? Who was the evil palm oil baron? Were they really working with wild animals? No, it must be circus animals they were using, or, at least, working elephants! Within only hours the whole of Malagiar was buzzing with talk, with speculation. The Prime Minister, in his office, was looking particularly grim.

"Tell the Defence Minister I want to see him immediately." he said to his Secretary.

"And then tell the palm oil baron I want to see him this afternoon, in my office. And notify Malagiar News that I shall be making a speech this evening."

Television crews and reporters from all manner of publication and television programmes were scrambling and jostling to find out where these children were, who they were. What was this story all about? What was really going on?

The children, blissfully unaware of the furore they had caused, went off early into the forest with Yusof and Professor Profundo. They carried herbs, salves and medicines for the animals. They were to meet the Orang Asli on the way to the glade where they would treat the animals.

Several animals were battered and bruised, but there were not too many actual wounds. Some had died in battle. That was sad, and the children were upset for them, but, as Yusof pointed out, they had not died in vain. Ibrahim and Joseph were particularly worried about Tunku and Matahari. Neither of them had complained, making light of their wounds, but they looked bad, and Ibrahim noticed that Tunku had difficulty using his right arm, and Matahari was hardly able to walk on his front right leg.

'They must be in such a lot of pain. I hope Bapa can help them.'

Yusof was worried about Matahari. If the bullets had lodged in his flesh, they would have to be dug out. That meant surgery! He had brought some local anaesthetic darts with him – just in case. He had already seen Tunku's wound. It was nasty, and would need stitches. He just hoped that none of the wounds had gone septic over night. But it had been impossible to see what he was doing last night and, above all else, he needed good light.

The evil palm oil baron was sitting in his office, looking disbelievingly at the newspaper spread out on his desk. He had read the article, every word of it, getting more and more agitated as he read. First, he had buried his head in his hands. He wanted to cry. Then he got angry. Now, his face was like thunder. What had gone wrong? Why had the Prime Minister intervened? How had the Press got hold of this? Where was Ah Kong? Ah Kong!

"Fetch me Ah Kong – now!" he screamed at the skinny office manager. "And burn all those e.mails."

The e.mails were flying in now, hundreds and hundreds of them, from all over the world, without exception telling him to leave the forest alone, not to be so greedy. They all condemned him.

'How dare they! How dare they! Those horrible children are responsible for this, I guarantee it. All this is their doing. And that Shirley Pooper woman – I shall sue her. I shall take her to the cleaners. I shall take her for everything she's got. And those children. I shall sue them too! I hate children. I hate them all!'

His face was a sort of purplish blue colour, his fat, greasy chins wobbled with his fury; his eyes were tight little slits, his pudgy hands were fidgeting, systematically breaking every pen or pencil he picked up. He stood up, he paced up and down, he kicked the desk.

"Ow!" he yowled. He hopped about on one foot, trying to clutch at the other. He had forgotten that he was wearing moccasins today. His secretary put a call through.

"I told you no calls" he screamed down the 'phone.

"This is the Prime Minister's Secretary speaking, Baron. He requests that you attend his office at 4.00 p.m. today. Can I tell him that you will be there?"

He blanched.

"Oh! Oh, yes, of course." he said, suddenly subdued.

'What does HE want? Well, of course, he was there. He cannot do too much damage; I have a tight hold on him. He will have to toe the line, do what I want him to do – or else I shall expose him. He knows that! I expect this is just a face saving exercise. Perhaps I can turn this to my advantage.'

The evil palm oil baron felt a little happier. Sitting down at his desk, he put his feet up, lit another large cigar, and telephoned his secretary, telling her to bring him a large coffee, and some sticky toffee pudding. He needed to cheer himself up. And then he would work out how to turn the interview with the Prime Minister to his own advantage.

The women in the kampong were cleaning up after the night before. The kampong was calm and orderly, just a few women cleaning, carrying things about. In the car park at the end of the street, there was a big commotion. Cars and vans were drawing up by the score. Men and women dressed in jeans and frequently with long hair and ear-rings, jumped out. They unloaded lots of equipment: cameras, tripods, videos, camcorders, loudspeakers, microphones, and lots more. They hurried down the main street, aggressive reporters followed by cameramen, questioning everyone as they went. Katak bounded around them, along with the other village dogs, barking furiously. Chickens, goats and buffalo scuttled out of their way. The villagers were proud, quiet people. They turned their backs on the intruders, pretending not to see them, or they responded quietly to shouted questions, shrugging their shoulders and pretending not to understand. Not even Aishah was at home; she had gone out to tend her precious seedling s and saplings.

The reporters held a small conference in the middle of the street, and decided that they would stay there and wait. This kampong was surely the one where everything had started. They made for the padang where they made themselves comfortable, sitting in the shade of the surrounding trees, and settled down to wait.

CHAPTER 21

In the forest glade, the animals were quiet. They knew that Yusof, the Orang Asli, and the children were there to help them. Some of them had severe wounds, but they did not complain. As Yusof approached them, speaking softly, they let him explore their wounds, clean them, dress them. The Orang Asli were great healers too, and they went about the business of bandaging little hands and paws which had been burned, dressing claws which had been torn out. There were many burns to be treated, cuts and gashes, and a few bullet wounds.

The children assisted. Faradilla found her special little civet cat. The pads on both its front and back paws were burned again. She had thought it would not get involved this time, having been burned before. It was such a brave little cat. She cuddled it, humming softly, while Ibrahim dressed the burns. The little civet cat, uncomplaining, snuggled up to Faradilla.

Xin Hui and Vinod made themselves useful applying bandages. Professor Profundo and Toby were watching the Orang Asli carefully. Their knowledge of the healing properties of forest plants was unique. Professor Profundo wanted to see how they used them, and Toby found himself just as fascinated as his father.

Tunku arrived. Puteri was with him this time, carrying their baby. She was worried about Tunku. Suddenly, he seemed old, tired. That gash in his shoulder was very deep, and he was in great pain. Ibrahim ran up to him, giving him a great hug. Tunku winced.

"Ayah, Ayah" Ibrahim called "Tunku is here. He needs your help."

Yusof finished bandaging the burned tail of the macaque he was dealing with, and came over to Tunku. They understood each other. Tunku turned round, presenting his right shoulder to Yusof. Yusof prodded it gently. The wound was deep, wide, and dirty. Yusof first had to cut the hair from around the wound, then he cleaned it out with spirit. Tunku winced, but Puteri was sitting next to him, holding tightly on to his hand, willing him through the pain. Then Yusof packed the wound with an antiseptic ointment he had prepared from the plants. He put a big dressing over it.

"I want to keep this wound open for a day or two" he said "to give all the dirt and infection a chance to get out. And then I shall have to stitch it. Ibrahim, can you tell Tunku that I really want him to come to the kampong and rest there, so that I can keep an eye on him."

Ibrahim spoke softly to Tunku, stroking his arm all the while. Tunku bowed his head and sat, staring at the ground for some time. When he looked up, his gaze was bleak.

"He does not want to come, Ayah. He wants to look after Puteri and the others. He is afraid the evil palm oil baron will still try to fire the forest."

Yusof looked at Tunku.

"I give you my solemn promise he will not. The forest is safe for the time being, and we are going to make sure that it remains safe for ever."

Tunku looked long and hard at Yusof. Then, raising himself heavily from the ground, he padded off slowly, knuckling the ground with his long arms, in the direction of the kampong. Puteri walked alongside him, still holding her baby. Number One Son followed, swinging through the branches overhead, but never far from his father.

Matahari's pain was intense, his wounds already badly infected. Lying on his side on the ground, he could scarcely raise his head. Ribut and Halilintar were gently trying to lift him up with their tusks. They had pushed their tusks under his front shoulder, and Rijaksana had pushed his tusks under Matahari's head, but he did not move. They stood around him, coiling their trunks around his, shaking their heads, swaying, rumbling encouragement to Matahari. When Yusof approached, they stepped back, giving him room. Ibrahim and Joseph were worried. Yusof examined the wound.

"This is serious. I am going to have to dig these bullets out. There are two, and they are spaced a good twenty centimetres apart. It seems one of them has chipped a bone, but it is not shattered. If I can get these out and clean the wounds sufficiently, Matahari should recover. But it will need a local anaesthetic. Can you tell Matahari, Ibrahim, that I shall have to dart him? Tell him his shoulder will be a little painful for a while afterwards."

While Ibrahim spoke to Matahari, stroking his trunk, Yusof called the Orang Asli over. He would need their help. Together, they darted Matahari and waited for him to go to sleep. Everybody was standing by, watching, waiting. Once Matahari was asleep, Yusof spun into action.

"We have not got much time. I have given his as little anaesthetic as possible. Too much would be dangerous. We have

probably got about fifteen minutes to find these bullets."

He and two of the Orang Asli climbed up on to Matahari's flank. First Yusof poured spirit over the wounds, then he inserted a sharp knife and probed the first wound. After only a few seconds, he grunted.

"I think I have got it." Carefully, he pulled the knife from the wound, and inserted his fingers. Slowly, precisely, he pulled out a bullet. He tossed it into a jar. Then he started work on the other wound, while one of the Orang Asli applied an evil smelling paste to the first wound. Yusof pulled out the second bullet, and the Orang Asli applied the evil smelling paste to that wound as well. Yusof looked at his watch.

"We have just one minute to go before Matahari comes round. Ibrahim, ask the other elephants to help him. It is essential he gets up on his feet."

Ibrahim spoke to the elephants. When Matahari awoke only seconds later, they all came forward and, with a strong united will, using tusks and trunks, they helped him up, first to a sitting position and then, when he had regained a little strength, they raised him to his feet. Joseph let out a long sigh of relief. He was quite sure he had held his breath throughout the operation. Matahari stood, shakily at first; the children cheered. Yusof and the Orang Asli smiled broadly, Professor Profundo tossed his hat in the air, and the elephants trumpeted their relief and delight.

"Tell them, Ibrahim, that he should be alright. They must take him as deeply into the forest as they can. He needs a lot of rest. And if there is any problem, they must come at once to me – or to the Orang Asli, and get help."

Ibrahim spoke again to the elephants. They rumbled. Turning, walking two on either side of Matahari, they headed off, deep into the forest, where he would rest undisturbed, and where Cahaya Bulan was waiting for him.

At last, all the animals were treated, and most were able to fend for themselves, but a few were very sick. The Orang Asli had brought their woven baskets and slings to carry the smaller animals, and they also had some stretchers for the bigger ones who could not walk. The biggest problem was burned feet; until they healed, they would just be too painful for walking.

And so they formed a sad little procession, carrying sick and wounded animals, in baskets, in slings, and on stretchers, heading back towards the kampong where Yusof would be able to look after them until they were well enough to fend for themselves. Faradilla carried her brave little civet cat. Xin Hui and Vinod each carried a couple of monkeys with burned hands and feet, Toby and Joseph carried a stretcher bearing a small bear with horribly burned paws, and Ibrahim carried a young leopard which had pulled some of its claws out, as well as burning its paws and its tail.

When they reached the edge of the kampong, they heard strange voices. They stopped, silent, wondering who they were. Tunku and Puteri emerged from the undergrowth. They had seen strangers, and were reluctant to enter the kampong. Putting the stretcher down very gently, Ibrahim and Joseph sat down to wait beside Tunku. The Orang Asli edged forward; the others waited. They came back and reported that there were many strangers waiting in the padang with photographic equipment.

"I was afraid this might happen". Yusof looked grim. "It is the reporters. I shall get rid of them. You must wait here. Be very quiet and still."

Straightening his shoulders, Yusof strode out of the forest. A stout stave in his hand, he headed up the path towards the padang When he arrived, the reporters clamoured for his attention, throwing question after question at him. He waited until they calmed down.

"As you all know, the whole story of what happened is in the South East Asia Gazette, I cannot add to that. There is nobody here. Please go. You are on private land, and have no right to be here."

Reluctantly the reporters got up and left, shouting that they would be back for more.

At last the sick animals could be bedded down. The children and Professor Profundo emerged from the forest. The Orang Asli melted away, as they always did.

Tunku sank gratefully on to a big bed of leaves that Puteri prepared for him. He fell into a deep sleep.

Yusof and Professor Profundo had a chat. They agreed that, now that so many reporters were involved, the best thing was for the children to give a News Conference.

∽∾∽∾∽∾∽∾∽∾∽∾

The Prime Minister was having a busy day. First, he had had a long and frank discussion with the Defence Minister. The Prime Minister was most concerned that the army were being used to support the Palm Oil Baron, fighting against villagers, women and children! Fighting against animals! What was the army coming to? Was this what countless millions of tax payers' money was spent on training the armed forces was for?

He asked the Defence Minister outright what "gifts" he had received from the Palm Oil Baron.

The Defence Minister, having nowhere to turn, owned up. He had accepted thousands of dollars in bribes, and presents from the Palm Oil Baron. Miserable, he offered his resignation with immediate effect. The Prime Minister accepted it.

"You will, of course, have your letter of resignation on my desk within the hour. Say that you are resigning for health reasons. That will save you some face! And I expect everything you have received from the Palm Oil Baron to be returned. I do not care how you do it, but do it! "

He turned, and walked out of the room. He did not even shake hands. The Defence Minister was left alone in the large room, feeling very small and inadequate. He was ruined! He would have to sell everything to repay the Palm Oil Baron, and his wife would be furious. She did like her little luxuries. He had no job, and, within days, would have no money either. Quietly, he slunk out of the room, and out of the building. Next, the Prime Minister had a meeting with the Palm Oil Baron. The first thing he did was to hand him a big cheque.

"I think that will account for all that my wife and I have ever received from your hands." he said coldly.

"But, My Dear Prime Minister, these were gifts. You have no need to pay me." The evil palm oil baron was ingratiating, grovelling. He smiled a sickly smile. He was sweating profusely, and wiped his brow with that large gold spotted silk handkerchief he always carried. He took the cheque, and put it in his breast pocket. The palms of his hands were damp.

"You should know that the Defence Minister has resigned, as will any other Minister you have bribed. I will not tolerate corruption in my government." said the Prime Minister. "I, myself, was foolish to accept gifts from you. But I have now paid my dues. I shall be making an announcement on air this evening."

The evil palm oil baron blanched. "What? What announcement, Prime Minister? Surely it does not have to come to this? We can resolve these silly issues. There is nothing here that cannot be cleared up."

CHAPTER 21

The Prime Minister looked at the evil palm oil baron. He did not say a word. 'How had this wretched man gained such power? How had HE, Teo, and many other of his Ministers become indebted to him?' The Prime Minister was disgusted with himself.

"Baron, you have enough plantations, and more, to last a lifetime. You do not need more. I have blocked your purchase of Black Rock island, and you will not be destroying any more forest. Is that understood?"

"Prime Minister, you are ruining me."

"That is as may be. I shall also be instructing my solicitors to sue you for bribery and corruption on the largest scale."

The evil palm oil baron was on his knees. "Prime Minister, I beseech you!" He was sobbing. "Boo-hoo, boo-hoo", blowing his nose loudly on that large gold spotted handkerchief again.

"Get up. This is preposterous. Good day, Baron." And the Prime Minister left the room, closing the door firmly behind him. His secretary appeared to escort the palm oil baron out of the building.

The evil palm oil baron could scarcely walk, his knees were shaking so badly. Head bowed, mopping his brow, pulling at his best gold tie, he was jibbering. "I am ruined! I am ruined!" The Prime Minister's secretary had to grasp his elbow to help him along, a chore he conducted with distaste! The Prime Minister's Secretary placed the evil palm oil baron in his car, and instructed the driver to take him home, where he would be kept under armed guard until his trial.

The Prime Minister then had a lengthy and serious meeting with his solicitor, after which he had an hour to rest and change, before meeting Professor Profundo, Yusof and the children. He knew very little about children; His own had grown up long ago, and he had been too busy working to pay them much attention. He had grandchildren, of course, but rarely had time to see them. He would have to rely on the Professor and Yusof for conversation.

❦❦❦❦❦❦❦❦❦

A big black shiny car arrived at the kampong. The driver was wearing a smart peaked cap. The children, dressed in their best clothes again, climbed in, accompanied by Yusof and Professor Profundo. They were a little nervous. They had never had dinner with a Prime Minister before. The Professor had told them to address the Prime Minister as Prime Minister the first time they spoke to him, but he said that after that they could address him as "Sir". That would be fine! Sitting in the car, Xin Hui was practicing.

"Prime Minister. Sir." under her breath, in case she got it wrong. Vinod sat quietly, fists clenched (he always did that when he was nervous). Faradilla was demure, hands folded in her lap. Ibrahim and Joseph were thoughtful. They were working out what they would say to the Prime Minister. Toby was thinking what a jolly time he and his Dad were having, and he was jolly glad they had come to Malagiar. Just wait till he got back to school and told all his friends.

The Prime Minister was waiting on the steps of his big house when they arrived. He, personally, opened the car door for them.

"Welcome to my humble abode" he cried, laughing. He escorted them up the white marble steps, surrounded by white marble columns, and chandeliers. They entered a magnificent entrance hall. Staff were standing discreetly everywhere.

"Perhaps you ladies might like to use the powder room" he said, smiling at Xin Hui and Faradilla.

"P.. Prime Minister, thank you, Prime Minister, Sir!" stuttered Xin Hui. The girls followed the maid who showed them where to go. They had to stand on tiptoe to reach the sheer glass hand basins to wash their hands. Surrounded by mirrors, with gold taps and soap dishes, fluffy white towels to hand, fresh flowers, and lovely sweet smelling soap and moisturizer, this was the smartest cloakroom the girls had ever been in.

When they returned, the boys were waiting for them. The Prime Minister was talking earnestly to Yusof and the Professor. Joseph, Ibrahim and Toby were gazing around them in awe. "Isn't this great!" whispered Toby, thoroughly enjoying himself. Vinod's eyes were wide. This was a palace!

Seeing that the girls had returned, the Prime Minister called "I hope everyone is hungry. I have asked the chef to lay on a feast for us today!" And he led the way into the dining room. They sat down in the chairs allocated to them. Someone had thoughtfully placed a cushion on Faradilla's chair, so that she could see over the top of the table. The feast the Prime Minister had laid on for them was magnificent. The boys ate and ate – as only boys can eat! The girls were very soon full.

The Prime Minister had been talking seriously with Yusof and Professor Profundo throughout the meal. Eventually he said, "I understand that you, Joseph, are the ring leader here." He smiled.

"Not exactly, Sir. We are all in this together. But I cannot stand by and watch the forest being burned down, the animals burning, suffering so horribly. I just feel I have got to help them. And the others feel the same. The Orang Asli are wonderful people, you know, and they are losing their homes."

"Yes, and there's so much in the forest for us all" chipped in Ibrahim. "The Orang Asli and the animals know all the secrets, and they can help us, if only we would take notice."

"I do not want the evil palm oil baron to burn down our kampong. I do not want to live in a high-rise. I want to keep my animals, my chickens, and Katak – that's my dog. The forest belongs to the Orang Asli and the creatures, and it's our forest too!" said Faradilla. "And I want the Orang Asli and the animals to feel safe in their own home, just as I want to feel safe in my own home."

"I've got a new baby brother, and I want him to know about the forest and the animals just as I do, and if it is all burned down, he will not get the chance."

"And I live in a high-rise, so Mummee says it would be unfair to have pets. But I do love the animals, and they are free in the forest. And, and, and even Mummee is not afraid of them any more." Xin Hui added softly.

"What do you think we should do about this, children?" asked the Prime Minister. He was looking very grave.

The children all looked at Joseph. Clearing his throat, he thought for a few minutes.

"I think, Sir, we all think. No, it is more than that. We all believe very strongly that the forest should be preserved, treated with respect, and the people and animals who live in it. Because they do not live as we do, it makes them no less than us. Actually, to know them makes our lives richer. I have driven with my Dad up and down the highways. You go for miles and miles and see nothing but palm oil plantations. Dad says that in the old days there were banana groves, pineapple groves, rubber plantations, paddy fields, gardens and kampongs. And now it is just palm oil." He spoke sadly. "When I grow up I do not want a world of only palm oil trees. I want the world to be as it should – balanced! Yes, that's the word. Balanced! There is no balance any more."

"Bravo, Joseph!" cried the Professor. "I could not have put that better myself. He is absolutely right, Teo. The world has to be balanced. How can we survive if it is not? We are already experiencing global warming on a massive scale. We are destroying our own planet. It has to stop."

"Prime Minister, why do you want to bring in more and more people to the country. Are there not enough already? More people will mean more burning forests, because they will think they need the land. But the land is not even used for planting crops, food. It is all being used for palm oil."

The Prime Minister looked in astonishment at Vinod.

"That was a big speech for a small boy! Let me try to explain. When a government is running a country, it needs money. People bring commerce and industry which, in turn, produces taxes and income for the government. Palm Oil brings a lot of income for the government. The government uses that money for the benefit of the people; it pays for the infrastructure of the land, roads, trains, airways, waterways, rivers, hospitals, housing, and so on, and it pays for the armed forces who protect us."

"But if we have fewer people, we will need less roads, trains, airways, and so on. We will need less armed forces to protect us. The more people there are, the more money the government will need." Xin Hui's logic was very simple.

"I do not want more people. I like things just as they are." Faradilla was passionate.

The Prime Minister, in the face of this simple logic, did not know what to say. '*What extraordinary children!*'

"Children, as we have finished dinner, there is something I have to tell you. We are going into another room in a minute, and I shall be making a speech for the media, who will all be there. There will be television cameras, flashing light bulbs, and all that sort of thing. You must not be frightened. But, after my speech, I would like you to answer any questions the press may put to you. The press will all be shouting questions at you at once, but I am sure that Yusof and Professor Profundo will field their questions. Answer them as openly and honestly as you have discussed matters here with me tonight. Do not be afraid." He smiled at them. It was a genuine, open smile. "You are quite famous now, you know."

He led them into a grand conference room, and showed them where to sit. They were placed on a dais, above the rows of chairs facing them. *'It is not so bad. It is just like when we were at the university'* thought Joseph. Doors at the far end of the room were flung open, and reporters streamed in. The Prime Minister was about to make an important speech. The future of the nation could be at stake. They pushed and jostled, striving to get the best seats. Not until they were seated did they look up and see the children on the dais. They realised at once that these were THE children, the children the South East Asia Gazette had been full of, and who they wanted so dearly to interview.

Excitement rippled, almost tangibly, through their ranks. Several stood up and started taking shots of the children. Faradilla and Xin Hui sat with their legs twisted around the legs of their chairs, holding hands, looking at each other, not to the front where all the reporters sat. Vinod, fists clenched as ever, studied his shoes very carefully. Ibrahim and Joseph looked serious, a little embarrassed, and Toby looked around him. He was having a great time! He dug Joseph in the ribs.

"Hey, Joseph, there's Shirley Pooper – and Bert!" Joseph looked, passed the word on to Ibrahim, who passed it on to Vinod, and he to the girls. They looked up. Shyly, they waved at Shirley and Bert, who waved happily back. The boys waved too. It lightened the atmosphere somehow, knowing that Shirley and Bert were there. The reporters were fidgeting and chattering, waiting for the Prime Minister, wondering what he was about to say.

The Prime Minister came in. They fell silent. Striding straight to a lectern in the middle of the dais, the Prime Minister, without preamble, started his speech.

"Ladies and Gentlemen. I have called you here today as a matter of urgency. This afternoon I tendered my resignation to the Cabinet."

The reporters gasped. They were shocked. What had happened?

The Prime Minister went on to explain that he had discovered several of his cabinet had been accepting bribes from the evil palm oil baron and that they had resigned. He explained that, indeed, he and his wife had accepted gifts from him, that he had now paid the evil palm oil baron for everything he had received, but that he felt it incumbent on himself to resign as Prime Minister of Malagiar. The evil palm oil baron was to be sued by the government for bribery and corruption.

Before he left office, however, he would ensure that, forever after, the forests of Malagiar were protected. No more forests were to be burned down – ever, for palm oil or for anything else. The people and the beasts of the forest, the plants of the forest were all, with immediate effect, under the protection of the Malagiar government. No more land was to be taken for the planting of palm oil. The government of Malagiar would now concentrate on re-establishing a balance in the land.

The children, Yusof and Professor Profundo were ecstatic. Vinod waved his clenched fist in the air "Yes!" he cried. Faradilla and Xin Hui gave each other a big hug. Faradilla was crying. She could not help it, she was so happy. For the first time that evening, Ibrahim and Joseph smiled. They laughed at each other, delighted. Ibrahim laughed at his father. Yusof, who had been very quiet all evening, looked as if a million tons had been lifted off his shoulders. And Toby shook his father's hand heartily. Professor Profundo was so thrilled, his big bushy eyebrows waggled up and down.

The Prime Minister suggested that the reporters might like to ask the children some questions – but not too many! And then he stepped down.

The reporters threw question after question at the children. What was it like in the forest? Were the animals that had helped them really wild? Could they really talk to the animals? Were there really Orang Asli in the forest, or were they just people dressing up?

The questions went on and on. Some of them were very silly. Then Shirley Pooper asked a question.

"The forest, thanks to your efforts, is now protected. What are you children going to do next?"

The children were silent. They had no idea. Ibrahim and Joseph shrugged.

"We shall go back to school, of course" Joseph said.

Yusof stood up.

"Ladies and gentlemen, I believe the children have had enough. Thank you for your time," he said. And with that, he herded the children off the dais.

He and Professor Profundo were much more concerned at the Prime Minister's resignation. He had been good at his job, albeit a little weak from time to time. What would become of Malagiar without him?

CHAPTER 22

The holiday had been exciting, exhausting, the best holiday ever, the children were agreed. The greatest pleasure had been in telling Tunku the forest was forever after protected.

Tunku had been tired and listless. Although his wound was healing nicely, he appeared to have given up. Everyone in the kampong was worried about him. When Ibrahim sat down beside him and Puteri, and told them what the Prime Minister had said, Tunku had not reacted immediately. Then, pulling himself up, he grinned a great big grin, from ear to ear, showing all his teeth. He rolled back on his back, and wriggled his whole body in delight. Then he turned a somersault, and another, and another. Puteri, rarely playful, rolled over and over, somersaulting with him. *'They are actually laughing. They are laughing, just like us,'* thought Joseph. As Tunku was still weak, Number One Son had been sent to tell Matahari the good news.

Yusof had been to see the Orang Asli. They would be very pleased. And Professor Profundo had been to see the Prime Minister. They both returned beaming. The Orang Asli were delighted, and the head man had declared that he and Yusof were eternally blood brothers – a high accolade indeed! And the Prime Minister told Professor Profundo that his cabinet, and therefore the people of Malagiar, had refused to accept his resignation, that he would remain, after all, as Prime Minister of Malagiar, but that he was more determined than ever to retain the forests and stamp out corruption. When Professor Profundo returned to Malagiar, which he promised to do very soon, perhaps they could spend a few days in the forest together, and the Professor could show the Prime Minister some of these wonderful plants he kept talking about.

It was the last evening before Toby and Professor Profundo flew home to the U.K. Aishah was giving them a small farewell party on the padang. Mr and Mrs Brown, Mr and Mrs Chan, and Mr and Mrs Singh had been invited. So had Shirley Pooper and Bert. Aishah had intended it to be a small party, but all the villagers joined in. They, too, were delighted with the outcome of all their efforts to save the forest and, indeed, the kampong itself. The grown ups were sitting together, talking, and laughing. Their whole lives had been changed in the past few days. The children were famous now, all over the world. They would have to take great care of them, protect them from too much exposure.

It was dusk, the fire flies were out and, in the distance, deep in the forest, they heard a great trumpeting, roaring, and shrieking. The sounds got louder and louder.

The children were sitting slightly apart from the grown-ups.

"It is Matahari" cried Ibrahim excitedly. He jumped up. "I recognise his voice. He's fine. He's well again! he shouted, whooping with glee."

Then Xin Hui recognised Cahaya Bulan's voice. "Mummee, Mummee" she called "Cahaya Bulan is calling goodbye."

Ibrahim and Tunku listened intently. "They are not calling good-bye." Ibrahim said. "They are celebrating, all the creatures are celebrating. The forest belongs to them again. They are happy."

For a long time everyone in the kampong listened, in awe and wonder, to the creatures of the forest.

"They are very special. It is our duty to protect them with all our might for the rest of our lives. We must talk to our teachers when we go back to school." Xin Hui said soberly.

Life is going to be very dull after this" Vinod said.

"Oh, I don't know" answered Joseph. "Have you seen all these e.mails? We are getting thousands of them. Look at this one." He started to read out "My name is Tomas. Can you help me with ....."

He was interrupted by Shirley Pooper.

"Bert and I have a small gift for each of you." She handed a package to each of them. And then she went over to the parents, and gave each of them a small package.

Ripping the paper off, the children had each been given a photograph:

Ibrahim sitting beside Tunku, Tunku's arm wrapped around Ibrahim. Joseph astride Matahari, Matahari's trunk raised in salute. Vinod on Ribut; Toby on Halilintar; Xin Hui on Cahaya Bulan. Faradilla stroking her beloved little civet cat.

The parents had been given photographs too, memorable moments! They were touched.

"Now, what are you kids going to do? You've got school next week, but then what? Whatever it is, Bert and I want to be there." Shirley laughed. "You will have to keep in touch, you know."

Joseph looked sideways at her. "Well, we are getting a lot of e.mails, most of them wanting help. Perhaps we shall find something else to do."

"I shall be writing a big article about the charity your Dads are setting up. I think that will be the next scoop." Shirley said happily.

THE END.

If You Wish to become a Member of

The Hallowed and Illustrious band of
The Doughty Warriors

Resolute, Courageous, Steadfast, and Valiant

Promising at all times to extend kindness, compassion and understanding to all creatures on this earth.

Promising to extend every effort to protect and preserve, to the best of your ability, all those creatures which swim in the seas, walk on the earth, or fly in the skies.

Promising to preserve and respect the trees, and all plants on this earth.

Promising to valiantly defend all life under the stars, however lowly.

You may enter the Doughty Warriors website: www.Doughtywarriors.com.

And enter your very own password, as below.

04067

Be sure to remember your password.

CHARACTERS

Joseph Brown & parents:	Mr & Mrs Brown
Vinod Singh & parents:	Mr & Mrs Singh
Chan Xin- Hui & parents:	Mr & Mrs Chan
Ibrahim Suleiman)	Parents: Yusof Suleiman
Faradilla Suleiman)	Aishah Suleiman
Katak	The dog
"The Evil Palm Oil Baron", Lee	Palm Oil plantation owner, who burns down the forest.
Ah Kong	The evil palm oil baron's overseer
Tunku Puteri	Orang Utan family
Matahari Cahaya Bulan Ribut Halilintar Bijaksana	Elephant
Hitam Malam	Moon Bear
Professor Profundo	Famous English Botanist.
Toby	his son
Shirley Pooper	second rate reporter
Bert	professional photographer
The Prime Minister (Teo)	

GLOSSARY OF TERMS

Abang	Term of endearment Literal meaning "Brother"
Almacida	Tropical tree
Anjung	Verandah
Attap	Palm whose leaves are used for roofing
Ayah	Father
Bapa	Father
Bijaksana	Wise/tactful
Biryani	Mild rice dish cooked with curried meat/chicken
Bomoh	Traditional healer
Cahaya Bulan	Moonlight
Cinchona	Tropical tree
Granthi	Sikh, custodian of the Adi Granth
Gurdwara	Sikh temple
Halilintar	Thunderbolt
Hitam Malam	Black night
Ibu	Mother
Kebaya	Blouse, often of thin, embroidered material
Kailan	Green vegetable
Kampong	Village
Katak	Frog
Kauri	Tropical tree
Mahogany	Hardwood tropical tree
Matahari	Sun
Mee Goreng	Fried noodle dish
Mee Siam	Noodle dish with spicy gravy
Mee soup	Noodle soup
Murtabak	Paper thin dough filled with curried, diced meat
Nasi Goreng	Mixed fried rice dish
Orang Asli	Native people
Padang	Field
Pak-choy	Green vegetable
Pharmacognosist	One who researches and creates medicines from natural sources (plants)
Puteri	Princess
Rambutan	a sweet tasting fruit with hairy skin
Ribut	Storm
Roti	Bread
Roti Prata	An Indian flat bread made from wheat flour and eaten with curry
Satay	Skewers of barbequed meat served with peanut sauce
Tofu	Soft, cheese-like cake made from soya beans
Tunku	Prince

THE AUTHOR

Influenced by her father's war-time diaries, observations of the African bush and life in the steaming tropical rainforests of Malaysia where much of her childhood was spent, Brenda has always been captivated by the power of description in the writing of others.

From the earliest age, she loved nature. As a child, she spent many happy hours in the African bush, and in the Malaysian forests, with binoculars, seeking out and observing the wild life. And she read copiously: Rudyard Kipling, Joseph Conrad, Somerset Maughan, Daniel Defoe and Thomas Hughes, among others.

Her adult career has been varied: advertising, sales and marketing, financial services, and even a small restaurant. But writing is her passion. *"If I go for a week without having written something, I feel deprived."*

Brenda's deep love of nature has prompted her to write "The Doughty Warriors" series. She hopes it will help children understand how important it is to preserve our planet, and to play their part in doing so.